LETHAL WEAPON

As the Hardys were passing the stone stairway that led up to the ground floor of the castle, the door at its top creaked open. Framed in the light was a huge man, staring down at them.

Moving much faster than a man his size usually did, he darted out a hand to grab something off the wall.

Frank sucked in his breath through his teeth when he saw what it was. Though rusty and covered with spiderwebs, the ancient battle-ax the man now held in his hands looked lethal enough to take care of both him and Joe.

Snarling in rage, the man charged toward them, swinging the ax like a baseball bat. The sharp edges sliced the air as he whipped the handle back and forth.

Frank and Joe had no choice—they had to retreat before the whistling blade got any closer. Unless the man got tired, they didn't stand a chance.

Books in THE HARDY BOYS CASEFILES® Series

#1	DEAD ON TARGET	#31	WITHOUT A TRACE
#2	EVIL, INC.	#32	BLOOD MONEY
#3	CULT OF CRIME	#33	COLLISION COURSE
#4	THE LAZARUS PLOT	#34	FINAL CUT
#5	EDGE OF DESTRUCTION	#35	THE DEAD SEASON
#6	THE CROWNING TERROR	#36	RUNNING ON EMPTY
#7	DEATHGAME	#37	DANGER ZONE
#8	SEE NO EVIL	#38	DIPLOMATIC DECEIT
#9	THE GENIUS THIEVES	#39	FLESH AND BLOOD
#10	HOSTAGES OF HATE	#40	FRIGHT WAVE
#11	BROTHER AGAINST BROTHER	#41	HIGHWAY ROBBERY
#12	PERFECT GETAWAY	#42	THE LAST LAUGH
#13	THE BORGIA DAGGER	#43	STRATEGIC MOVES
#14	TOO MANY TRAITORS	#44	CASTLE FEAR
#15	BLOOD RELATIONS	#45	IN SELF-DEFENSE
#16	LINE OF FIRE	#46	FOUL PLAY
#17	THE NUMBER FILE	#47	FLIGHT INTO DANGER
#18	A KILLING IN THE MARKET	#48	ROCK 'N' REVENGE
#19	NIGHTMARE IN ANGEL CITY	#49	DIRTY DEEDS
#20	WITNESS TO MURDER	#50	POWER PLAY
#21	STREET SPIES	#51	CHOKE HOLD
#22	DOUBLE EXPOSURE	#52	UNCIVIL WAR
#23	DISASTER FOR HIRE	#53	WEB OF HORROR
#24	SCENE OF THE CRIME	#54	DEEP TROUBLE
#25	THE BORDERLINE CASE	#55	BEYOND THE LAW
#26	TROUBLE IN THE PIPELINE	#56	HEIGHT OF DANGER
#27	NOWHERE TO RUN	#57	TERROR ON TRACK
#28	COUNTDOWN TO TERROR	#58	SPIKED!
#29	THICK AS THIEVES	#59	OPEN SEASON
#30	THE DEADLIEST DARE	#60	DEADFALL
		#61	GRAVE DANGER
		#62	FINAL GAMBIT
		#63	COLD SWEAT
		#64	ENDANGERED SPECIES
		#65	NO MERCY

Available from ARCHWAY Paperbacks

THE HARDY BOYS CASEFILES NO. 44

CASTLE FEAR

FRANKLIN W. DIXON

AN ARCHWAY PAPERBACK
Published by POCKET BOOKS
New York London Toronto Sydney Tokyo Singapore

AN ARCHWAY PAPERBACK *Original*

An Archway Paperback published by
POCKET BOOKS, a division of Simon & Schuster Inc.
1230 Avenue of the Americas, New York, NY 10020

Copyright © 1990 by Simon & Schuster
Cover art copyright © 1990 Brian Kotzky
Produced by Mega-Books of New York, Inc.

ISBN: 0-671-74615-4

First Archway Paperback printing October 1990

10 9 8 7 6 5 4 3

THE HARDY BOYS, AN ARCHWAY PAPERBACK
and colophon are registered trademarks of Simon & Schuster Inc.

THE HARDY BOYS CASEFILES is a trademark
of Simon & Schuster Inc.

Printed in the U.S.A.

IL 6+

CASTLE FEAR

Chapter

1

"THIS FOG gives me the creeps." Joe Hardy's broad, usually smiling face was creased in a frown as he peered into the thick murk around him. "Anybody could be lurking in this stuff five feet away from us and we wouldn't have a clue."

The narrow two- and three-story town houses along the cobblestoned lane were blurred in the heavy mist. The only tinge of color Joe caught came from the dozens of small lighted windows— yellowish rectangles floating in the air.

This was a fashionably old-fashioned section of London. The Hardys, eighteen-year-old Frank and Joe, who was a year younger, had parked their rented car just off Fulham Road and were heading for the temporary home of their lat-

1

est client. The fog was rolling in from the Thames River, a few blocks to their right, causing Frank and Joe to zip up their lightweight windbreakers against the dampness.

"You could hide an army in this soup." Joe ran a hand through his slightly damp blond hair. "Why can't it just decide to rain? We'll probably be bumping into Jack the Ripper next."

His older brother's dark eyes glinted with suppressed laughter. "I sort of like the fog."

"Why?"

"Well, we're in London. And London is famous for its fog."

"It's also famous for its fish and chips. And I'd rather bump into a batch of those right now." Joe hunched his broad shoulders in his jacket. "This continual mist is getting me down."

"Maybe our new case will cheer you up."

"Right," said Joe. "But I was expecting some fun, at long last. We didn't have much, studying our brains out for those summer courses at Oxford—there were those guys trying to *blow* them out, too." In the Hardys' last adventure, *Strategic Moves,* they had not only studied at the famous university, they'd broken up a kidnap plot designed to destroy East-West relations.

"I know what you mean," Frank admitted. "But that old friend of Dad's out in Hollywood needed some help. Since Dad's got that case in

South America and we're right on the spot, it's up to us.''

"Right, right. The family tradition.''

Fenton Hardy, their father, was a private investigator of international renown. Frank and Joe were pretty good detectives in their own right, and they'd often handled cases their father was too busy to attend to. That was once again the situation tonight.

"Keep in mind that working on a case is also probably better for your health,'' Frank pointed out. "Since your idea of fun always includes eating an entire pizza by yourself and then topping it off with—''

He was interrupted by the harsh crack of a pistol shot somewhere nearby. A slug whizzed past, close enough for Frank to feel the breeze of its passing whip through his dark hair.

He dived to the sidewalk and rolled. Joe hit the ground and stretched out flat.

Another shot came whistling their way, but it passed harmlessly through the space where they'd been a few seconds earlier.

Very quietly Joe asked, "What was that you were saying about this being healthy work?''

Seconds passed, but there were no further shots. As Joe was pushing himself up off the damp pavement he caught a glimpse of someone running off about half a block away. The swirling fog swallowed up the dark figure an instant after Joe had spotted it.

3

"I think I see something." Joe got to his feet.

"Joe, don't go chasing after an armed attacker."

"Catch you later," Joe said as he started to run along the foggy London lane.

The heavy gray mist seemed to disperse as he ran through it, spinning away into wispy tatters and then closing in behind him again.

He was straining to hear. From up ahead he thought he could make out the sound of hurrying footfalls, but everything was muffled and indistinct.

Then the running footsteps abruptly died. Joe heard only the sound of his own feet slapping the sidewalk.

He kept running, staring into the mist, his blue eyes narrowed.

Suddenly he was falling.

Something unseen on the ground had tripped him. Joe's left knee hit the pavement first, sending a painful jolt up his thigh as he went sprawling.

He shook his head ruefully and started to get up. Halfway to his feet, he paused.

Joe pivoted, then went charging toward a shadowy doorway on his right. He hurried up the five stone steps and grabbed.

"I'd rather you didn't do that."

He let go of the dark-clad figure, moving back a pace. "Sorry. I didn't expect a—uh, young woman. What are you doing in there?"

"Minding my own business, which is more than I can say for you."

There was some light, though dim, coming through the stained-glass window in the upper half of the oaken door the young woman was leaning against. She was a pretty girl, about the same age as Joe. Her hair was a wild mass of red curls, and the angry flush didn't hide the sprinkle of freckles on her high cheekbones. Hazel eyes flashed at him. The girl wore a black raincoat and a navy blue scarf. Both of her hands gripped a huge black shoulder bag.

Joe glared right back at her. "Somebody took a potshot at my brother and me."

"Maybe he had a good reason. If you go around tackling innocent bystanders, you're bound to make enemies."

"I never saw an innocent bystander hiding out in a doorway before."

"Me? Hiding out?" the girl said. "I heard those shots and ducked in here."

"And what are you doing out here in the first place?"

"If you must know, I'm walking a dog."

Joe glanced around. "What dog?"

"His name is Bozo, and he belongs to the people I'm staying with," the girl replied. "But now he seems to have run off."

"Have you seen anyone else, somebody who went running by?"

"It's tough to see anything in fog like this."

"Hear anything?"

"Just the shots, then you doing a bellyflop on the cement."

Joe was staring down at her shoulder bag. "I know I saw someone, a figure running this way."

Sighing, the red-haired girl yanked the bag wide open. "Take a look if you think I have a gun in here," she invited.

Joe leaned and looked. He saw a 35-millimeter camera and a small cassette recorder, but no sign of a gun. "Listening to you speak," he said, "I wouldn't say you sound British."

"Neither do you."

"I'm American. What's your excuse?"

"Same as yours. I'm from Connecticut, over here on vacation. Some friends of mine are putting me up at an apartment nearby." She looked anxiously out at the dense fog. "If all the excitement is over for the night, I'd better find poor Bozo."

"I don't know if you should be walking alone at this time of night, with a gunman on the loose," Joe said.

But the girl seemed anxious to leave. "I have friends expecting me, and I'm already late. I'd better hurry."

Joe nodded slowly. "I guess you'd better."

"Nice meeting you." She smiled faintly before brushing past him and starting along the sidewalk, calling, "Bozo, where are you? C'mon, boy. Wouldn't you like a nice bone? Bozo, Bozo . . ."

Very soon she was lost in the mist.

Joe watched until the girl had disappeared. Now, why do I have a hard time believing that Bozo really exists? he asked himself.

Shrugging, he retraced his steps. He walked a little slowly. Why rush when he knew he'd have to put up with a lecture from Frank about how dumb it was to go chasing gunmen?

Joe wasn't too happy with himself, either. He'd gone charging off after danger and had only caught a redhead—and an unfriendly one at that. She was cute, though, he had to admit to himself.

Too bad she was probably a liar. Joe had a strong suspicion she'd been putting him on, yet he couldn't believe she was actually the person who'd fired at him and Frank.

He got back to where they'd hit the dirt, but Frank wasn't around.

Moving along another quarter of a block, Joe spotted his brother in the doorway of a large brick town house. Frank seemed to be looking into the shadowy entryway and was hunched over oddly.

"Hey, Frank," Joe called. "Why are you standing that way? You hurt?"

"Not exactly." His brother answered without turning. "It's mostly because this gentleman here has a gun jammed into my stomach."

7

Chapter

2

FRANK STARED DOWN at the gun, a flashy chrome-plated revolver. The man holding it with the barrel pressed into Frank's middle was about forty. He was short, deeply tanned, and not dressed for the chilly, misty London night. He was clad in prefaded jeans, a flamboyant yellow-and-red Hawaiian shirt, and white tennis shoes.

"Come where I can see you, kid," the man told Joe, looking out around Frank. "Don't make any sudden moves, don't try to pull a piece on me—or your pal here buys the farm."

Frank managed a glance over at his approaching brother. "I've been trying to explain to this gentleman that—"

"You can't con me," interrupted the guy with the gun. "I'm turning both of you over to the

London Metropolitan Police. I'll prove these crimes aren't a publicity stunt. As if somebody of Larry Berman's stature in the industry would try the old 'somebody's threatening my client' bit."

He puffed up his chest. "Hey, does Larry Berman—one of the slickest agents in Hollywood—need cheapo publicity stunts to promote a respected young actor like Jed Shannon? No way, friends, nope, not at all. His last film, *Slam Dancin' in Rio,* broke all the records—"

"Mr. Berman," Joe managed to get in, "we weren't behind that shooting you heard."

"Oh yeah? Soon as I heard the shots—another of your cheap scare tactics—I grabbed my piece and ran out here. And who do I find skulking in the pea soup? This shifty-looking guy."

"Does the name Fenton Hardy mean anything to you?" asked Frank.

"Once I show you hoods to the cops, they'll realize Ted is in real danger and that I'm not—What was that name?"

"Fenton Hardy is our father." Frank pulled back a little from the gun barrel. "He's a well-known detective."

Joe added, "A producer friend of his named Norman S. Lenzer wanted him to—"

"Normie, sure. He produced Jed's latest blockbuster, *A Punk at Oxford.* That's why we're in this country—to promote the picture.

But I'm telling you, almost as soon as we're off the plane—bam!—trouble begins."

"That's why we're here. Our father's busy with a case in South America, so Joe and I are going to handle this for you."

"How are a pair of London street hoods going to help Jed Shannon?"

Joe sighed. "We're not street hoods, Mr. Berman. We're not even from London."

Berman lowered his gun. "This isn't a scam you're trying to pull on me?"

"I'm Joe Hardy, he's Frank Hardy. We have an appointment to see you and your client, Jed Shannon, at nine o'clock tonight."

The tanned agent frowned. "We are supposed to be meeting with the Hardys," he admitted. "But why were you popping those guns off?"

"We weren't. Somebody shot at us, and I took off to chase the person. Meanwhile, Frank— What *were* you doing, Frank?"

"Approaching the house here, and hoping you weren't off getting shot. Dumb move, Joe."

"Not if I'd caught him—or her."

"Hey, fellas." Berman put down his gun. "Suppose I see some ID. You— Frank, is it?"

"I'm Joe."

"Fine. Slowly and nonthreateningly, slip out your credentials."

Joe took his wallet out of his hip pocket and opened it to his driver's license. "Here you go."

"From Bayport, huh? Sounds like a real hick

town." The agent tucked the gun into the waistband of his jeans. "Sorry I gave you guys a bad time. I've been pretty stressed out lately."

Frank shrugged. "Suppose we go inside and talk about why?"

"Good idea." Berman gestured at the door behind him. "Anything to get out of this London fog. Give me Hollywood any day."

Jed Shannon was a dark, handsome young man in his early twenties, slim and about five foot ten. As he paced the living room of his rented town house, his clenched fists were jammed in the pockets of a black jacket, which he wore over a white T-shirt and black jeans. "It's reality time, Larry," he said to his agent. "I'm a big boy now, and I don't need guarding like some—"

"Kid, you can't go running out into the street—especially in a strange city—to go chasing after a gunman. That's why I went."

"You sure didn't do such a great job." Shannon stomped past the glass and metal coffee table. "You act like I'm some ninety-seven-pound weakling. Then you drag home a couple of overgrown Boy Scouts to hold my hand."

"Well, Shannon, if you don't think you need us . . ." Joe began.

"He needs you, he needs you." Berman wrung his hands. "I want professional help. I don't want this guy's life in danger."

11

"Larry, you forget that I grew up in the toughest part of Detroit." The actor slammed his hand on the mantelpiece. "I have street smarts. At least I did till you people started treating me like some kind of wimp who can't fight his own battles."

"I thought you grew up in Grosse Pointe," Joe suddenly said. "That's not exactly the toughest Detroit neighborhood. It's where the car-company millionaires and their rich kids live."

Shannon stopped pacing and scowled at Joe. "Okay, maybe my parents were pretty well off," he admitted. "But I learned from the tough kids I hung out with how to handle myself. If you care to test that, just let me know."

"Instead of everybody trying to prove who's toughest," Frank said calmly, "why don't you tell us what's been going on? At least then we could give you some advice."

The young actor glanced at him. "Which one are you—Tom or Jerry?"

"Frank Hardy."

Joe shot to his feet with a disgusted glare at Shannon. "C'mon, Frank, let's hit the road. This guy doesn't want us around."

"This is a job we told Dad we'd tackle," his brother reminded him. "We made a promise to protect him, not to become his best friend."

"But *everybody* likes Jed," insisted Berman. "Didn't you see the latest poll in *Fanteen,* where they voted him the—"

"I don't need protecting—or anybody to wipe my nose." Jed scowled at his agent.

"Jed, cool it," advised Berman.

"Just tell us what's been happening," suggested Frank. "Joe, sit down someplace."

"I'd rather be sitting down in a pizzeria on the other side of London." Joe stalked over to a large black armchair and sat down.

Shannon said to Frank, "Obviously, you're the rational one on the team."

Frank lowered himself into a white canvas chair. "Can you at least outline the problem?" he asked, glancing from the actor to the agent. "Then we can figure out what has to be done."

Berman glanced uneasily over at his angry client and asked, "You want me to tell them, kid?"

The younger actor shook his head. He walked over to stare into the empty stone fireplace. "I'm fairly sure this is just some crank thing," he began. "You two guys may not think much of me as an actor, but in the past year or so I've become what you'd call a celebrity. That means a lot of media hype. Interviews on the talk shows, photo sessions for the magazines . . ."

"*Celeb* magazine just voted him one of the Ten Hottest Hunks in Hollywood," the agent cut in.

"I'll tell the story, Larry."

"Detectives need these little background details," Berman said.

13

Shannon sighed. "Stars get a lot of attention. Unfortunately, some of it comes from people who are borderline crazies. That means some hate mail, a nut phone call now and then, a few threats. Mostly it's harmless. Annoying, sure, but not all that dangerous."

"That's not always true," said Frank. "There have been cases, you know, where obsessed fans have killed or seriously hurt stars."

"Is that what's happening here?" Joe asked the agent. "Are we talking about a crazed fan?"

Shannon answered. "I'm not sure who this person is. We've been in London for five days to promote *A Punk at Oxford*. You know, dozens of half-witted radio and TV interviews, equally stupid magazine and newspaper stuff, personal appearances. Tomorrow night, for example, I've got a boring speech to make to a bunch of European movie distributors. By the way, Larry, the opening three paragraphs of that speech will have to be changed."

"Kid, Normie Lenzer himself okayed that speech. We can't change a word without his okay."

"So get his okay. I'll give you my ideas for a new opening, and you fax them to him in L.A."

Frank cleared his throat. "What about the threats?"

Shannon continued. "Three days ago, while I was driving my Jaguar, someone in a car tried to force me off the road and down a rocky hill-side. Could have been just a chance thing, but the next day somebody shot at me—three times with a rifle, by the sound of it—while I was out jogging on the Embankment.''

''The phone calls.'' Berman sounded as though he were coaching the actor in a scene.

''I've also gotten two nasty phone calls.''

''What sort of caller?'' Frank wanted to know.

''Some whispering voice said I was marked for death unless I got out of London right away.''

''Did they claim responsibility for the shots and the car business?'' Joe asked.

The actor replied, ''Yeah, the second call did. Something like, 'We'll keep trying until you get tired and head for home.' ''

''The letter,'' coached Berman.

''Right. There was a letter, printed in pencil on cheap notebook paper. It had the same kind of message—that I'd get seriously hurt if I didn't leave town.''

''Can we see the note?'' asked Frank.

''Afraid not.'' The actor shook his head. ''I tore it up and flushed it.''

''I told him that was the kind of stuff the police needed. How else could they catch this nut case?''

Frank said, ''You've seen the police, then?''

Berman nodded vigorously. ''Twice. They did send a couple of detectives, but . . .'' He shrugged. "I could tell they thought I was trying for some cheap publicity."

Joe glanced over. "Have you gotten free publicity out of these attacks and threats?"

"You saying we actually rigged this for some coverage?" Berman shot back.

"No, I mean, has any of this wound up in print or on television?"

"We've been able to keep it quiet," said the agent. "If people get the idea Jed has people around who don't like him, it hurts his image."

Frank leaned forward. "You didn't recognize this voice on the phone, Jed?"

"No."

"Man or woman?"

"I'd say a man."

"What about the handwriting on the note?"

"Just scribbling in block letters."

Joe stood up. "It's improbable that a fan could have known your phone number." He walked to one of the bow windows in the room, looking into the foggy night below. "The person who made those calls needed some way to get that number."

Berman blinked. "I never thought of that."

Shannon just shrugged. "We gave it to all kinds of media people. It's not exactly a secret."

"But to get it, you'd need a media connection," Joe pointed out.

Shannon's smile was bitter. "Some media

people would probably sell the number for a few bucks."

"Is there anybody you can think of—anyone you know personally—who might want to threaten you?" asked Frank.

"Hey." Jed raised his eyebrows mockingly and struck a pose. "Larry just told you that everyone on earth loves me." Then he shook his head. "I really can't come up with the name of anybody in England who's got a grudge against me."

Frank turned to the agent. "You don't suspect anyone?"

"I think it's more than just a disgruntled fan. Something more serious than that."

"About the shots tonight," Joe said. "Who knew we were due to come over here?"

"No one—except me and Jed."

Frank nodded. "Then I want to check the phones before we leave tonight."

"You think they're bugged?"

"That's one way to find out Jed's itinerary *and* know that we were coming here at nine."

"It could simply be that somebody was out there watching this place," Shannon objected. "When you two came by, they recognized you and took a couple of potshots."

Frank said, "Maybe, except—"

The phone rang.

Berman jumped to his feet and hurried to the glass-topped phone stand near the windows.

"Yes?" He listened for a second, then turned to Frank. "It's for you."

"Who is it?"

"Didn't say."

Frank got up and took the receiver. "Frank Hardy speaking."

A very cultured British voice came over the line. "We missed you and your brother this time, young man."

"Who is this?" Frank demanded.

The voice went on as if he hadn't spoken. "If you hope to live to become an old boy, don't help young Mr. Shannon. Tell him to give up his search for Jillian."

Chapter

3

FRANK HUNG UP. Then he lifted the receiver again, quickly unscrewed the mouthpiece, and removed a small electronic device—a bug. He looked toward Jed Shannon and said, "Can you tell me who Jillian is?"

The actor started as if the fireplace had suddenly burned him. "Who was that on the phone?"

"I have no idea. But whoever he was, he sure doesn't want us to help you find Jillian."

Joe asked, "Does this tie in with your gunman?"

"You got it," Frank replied. "Unless we drop the case, the next shots won't miss."

"Then suppose you tell us who she is," Joe said to the actor.

Berman sank low in his chair. "You might as well, kid."

"If any of this winds up in some scandal tabloid," warned Shannon, "I'll—"

"Before you go further," cut in Frank, "I'd better explain something. Unless you feel you can trust Joe and me, there's no use trying to do business with us."

"But if we do tackle your case," added Joe, "then you're really going to have to tell us the truth."

"Do it, kid," said Berman.

Shannon sat on a long, low black leather sofa and ran a hand over his face. "I shouldn't have been screaming at you guys. But this whole situation has me a little hyper."

He sighed. "I guess it began about ten months ago, doing the location shooting for *A Punk at Oxford*. I met a girl. Her name is Jillian Seabright—yeah, that's her real name. She's an actress, a very good one. Nobody's ever heard of her in the States because she's mostly done stage work and a little television here in London. Jillian had a small role in my movie, which is how I met her."

Frank asked, "Did you date her?"

"Not exactly. Nothing formal, anyway. We had lunch once or twice at an out-of-the-way inn she knew about, and we mostly just sat around and talked for hours. You know how it is when you really hit it off with someone. We became friends, actually."

"Jillian really isn't like any of the actresses I've known," he explained. "She doesn't seem like a show business person at all. She's bright, caring, and—I just like her." He rose up, pacing again. "Fact is, it wasn't until I was back home in Los Angeles that I realized how *much* I liked her. So I started calling her long distance."

"Expensive," commented Joe.

"I can afford it, and Jillian is worth it." The actor gave them a sheepish shrug. "She's a very special sort of girl. Anyway, we agreed that when I came over here to promote the opening of my movie in England, we'd get together."

"I nearly had to tie him down to keep him from hopping over here weeks ago to see her," Berman chipped in. "That would have fouled us up with promoting *A Punk at Oxford*. We were nearly number four at the box office for almost—"

"Enough, Larry."

Frank asked the actor, "So what happened when you got to England?"

Shannon shook his head. "I didn't find her."

"Wasn't she expecting you?" Joe frowned.

"Sure she was. I talked to her on the phone just a few days before I left L.A."

"She didn't hint that anything might be wrong?"

"Nothing like that. We had a dinner date set

for my first night in town.'' Shannon dropped onto the sofa. "But I couldn't get any answer to my phone calls. Then I went over to her flat in the St. Marylebone district, and she wasn't there."

"What did they tell you at her building?" asked Frank.

"A neighbor said Jillian is still living there. I mean, she didn't move out or anything. But nobody had any idea where she's gone to."

"The kid's tried everything he can think of," said the agent. "The West End theater where she was doing a play, the—"

"What happened at the theater?" asked Joe.

Shannon replied, "Jillian had a small part in this Restoration comedy called '*Tis a Pity She Won't Be Woo'd*. But she'd been replaced, and nobody knew where she'd gone off to."

"When's the last time she was in the play?" Frank asked.

"She did the part till about three days before I got to town."

Frank said, "Does she have an agent?"

"Some seedy guy named Ian Fisher-Stone," said Shannon. "I checked with him, too, over the phone, and he didn't know a thing."

"You mean," said Frank, "he had a client working and didn't even wonder why she quit a play and disappeared?"

"Fisher-Stone told me Jillian was just off on a holiday. But he didn't know where she'd gone."

"How did he know she went on a vacation?"

"He wasn't very clear on that, but he gave me the impression it wasn't Jillian herself who told him."

Frank looked closely at Jed. "I don't want to set you off again, but is it possible she has another boyfriend?"

"She told me she didn't, not anyone serious."

"Did she mention anything else to you?" Frank continued. "Somebody who was annoying her? Or maybe some out-of-town acting job that might be coming up?"

Shannon started to shake his head, then stopped, frowning. "Wait now," he said. "She did tell me once or twice that maybe she was going to be a star, too. She didn't give me any details, but I had the idea she was probably being considered for a big part in a movie or play."

"You didn't know what it was, though?" Frank asked.

"She didn't give more than hints. Lots of actors and actresses are very superstitious, and they won't talk about a big part until after they've signed for it."

"Even if she has a part in a big-budget movie," said Joe, "that doesn't explain why people are threatening you."

"And Jillian *is* involved in the threats—right?" asked Frank.

Jed Shannon sighed. "Yeah. Both the phone

23

calls and the letter warned me to forget about Jillian."

Eyes narrowing, Frank glanced from Jed to Larry Berman. Something was wrong with this case, right from the start. "There's got to be more to this than what I'm hearing here. This girl didn't just go off to star in a movie."

"I'll tell you what I'm afraid of," said Shannon. "That's she's been kidnapped or something, and that I'll never see her again."

Frank said, "This doesn't sound like a kidnapping."

"What do you mean? She's vanished, and nobody can find her."

Frank gave him a long, hard look. Shannon seemed sincerely upset, but actors—even bad actors—could be hard to read. "Kidnappers do it for money," he said, probing. "Here you are, a guy making a huge salary. Instead of trying to scare you off, the bad guys should be hitting you up for a fat ransom."

"What about her family and relatives?" said Joe. "Could be they've been approached about a ransom."

"No. Jillian's an orphan. There's no family at all."

Frank said, "All that's clear right now is that wherever Jillian Seabright is, there's somebody who doesn't want her found."

Shannon asked, "But why?"

"That's what we'll have to find out." Frank

rose up. "We'll need all those addresses. Her home, the theater, her agent."

"I've already checked all those out," Shannon said.

"But we haven't." Joe got to his feet, too. "And how about a photo?"

Shannon shook his head. "I don't have one," he said, a little embarrassed. "Well, I have a dozen, actually, but I left them all at my beach house in Malibu."

"What does she look like?" Frank asked.

"She's very pretty."

"Can you get a little more specific?"

Shannon closed his eyes. "Five foot four, about a hundred and ten pounds, blond hair, shoulder length. Jill's got a heart-shaped face, dimples, big eyes. They're . . . they're . . . well, sort of gray-green." He looked a little flustered as he opened his eyes. He took a big breath and said, "I really am worried about her."

"We'll find her," Joe assured him.

"Now, let's take a look at these phones," said Frank.

The fog was even denser when the brothers left Jed Shannon's town house. It closed in tight around them as they started walking back toward their car.

Joe said, "Think we'll be able to trace that bug you found in the phone?"

"Probably not."

"Maybe we ought to persuade Shannon to go to the police again."

Frank said, "You heard me suggest that to Larry Berman. But he's convinced the London police think he's just a publicity nut."

"We've got evidence now, since that bug was real."

"We've only got evidence that there was a bug on the phone." Frank shook his head. "There's no way of proving who planted a snooping device there."

"Meaning Berman himself could have done it?"

"I don't think he did, Joe, but the police might."

After walking a few paces in silence, Joe remarked, "I hope we find Jillian Seabright."

His brother grinned. "That's part of our job now," he said. "Find her, and we should find whoever is threatening Jed Shannon. But you sound like you have other motives."

"Hey, I'd just like to meet the lady," said Joe. "Think about it, Frank. A multimillion-dollar Hollywood actor like Jed Shannon must meet dozens of incredible girls every day. You know—actresses, models, heiresses, maybe even a princess or two."

"True." They'd reached their parked car, and Frank fished the keys from his pocket.

"*But* he flies all the way to London from far-off California to see this one girl again," Joe said.

Unlocking the door on the driver's side, Frank said, "He had to come to London anyway. He's promoting his new movie." He slid in behind the wheel, reaching across to open Joe's door.

"No, I think he really is in love with Jillian. You could hear it in his voice."

"He's an actor. He can make you hear anything in his— What's the matter, Joe?"

Joe held out a file card to his brother. "I just found this on my seat."

Neatly lettered on the white card were six words.

This could have been a bomb.

Chapter
4

"WELL, THAT WAS considerate of someone to give us such a break," Joe said with a smirk. "I wonder if this was put in the car before or after we were shot at."

"Whoever it was must have dropped it in through the crack in your window," Frank said as he started the car. "Maybe it was put there by the person I had that nice chat with on the phone."

"Or a certain red-haired girl who lost her dog," Joe mused.

Frank took his eyes off the road to look quizzically at his brother. "What are you talking about?"

As they made their way to the hotel Joe told

his brother of his encounter with the girl in the doorway.

When they let themselves into their room Frank took the card from Joe and inspected it. "Too bad Jed got rid of that letter telling him to leave town. We have no way of knowing if this was written by the same hand."

The Hardys left their hotel, a grand but faded palace just off the Strand, early the next morning. The new day was chilly and gray, and a light rain was falling. In search of a heartier meal than the continental breakfast their hotel offered, Frank and Joe followed the concierge's directions and, a few minutes later, were having breakfast in a quaint hotel restaurant on a street off Trafalgar Square.

The place was decorated in yellows and greens, and a thick, rich carpet kept things quiet, absorbing the clatter of knives and forks, teacups and plates, and the conversations of the numerous diners.

In spite of the grand surroundings, Joe frowned down at his plate. "This doesn't look much like an English muffin."

"We're in England, the headquarters of English muffins." Frank dipped his toast into the yolk of his fried egg. "They must know how to make the things."

"You'd think so, wouldn't you?" Joe spread more marmalade on a muffin half. "But this isn't anything like the English muffins you get at the supermarket back home in Bayport."

Frank cut a slice of bacon and grinned. "Joe Hardy, the well-traveled tourist."

"I happen to be an expert on English muffins." Joe spread more marmalade. "Any new thoughts on this case occur to you during the night?"

"No, I still think we have to start by locating Jillian Seabright. She's the key to all this."

"Jed's studio is going to have two security people going along with him on his round of interviews today," said Joe around a mouthful of muffin. "So we're covered on that."

Frank didn't look so sure. "The bad guys—if that's what they are—have been pretty good at getting around security measures."

Joe leaned back in his chair. "I don't think you're completely sure this isn't just a publicity gimmick."

"I'm just not a hundred percent certain Jed's in love with this missing girl."

"Maybe not, but if this was a publicity thing, they'd have gotten something into the papers," Joe pointed out. "I bought an armload of them, from stately to sleazy, when we got back to the hotel last night. Several mentions of Jed and his movie, sure, but not a word about Jillian."

"This is a natural for the *Daily Yell*. 'Star Searches for Lost Love. Fame and a New Film

Can't Ease Heartbreak.' You know the kind of headlines this story will generate," Frank said.

"I'm betting Jillian really is in some kind of trouble, and that Jed doesn't have any idea where she is."

Frank took his last mouthful of egg, wiped his mouth with a cloth napkin, and asked for the check. "After today, maybe we'll have some answers."

"Sure you're okay on the way we're splitting up the work?"

With a nod, Frank said, "I'll track down Jillian's agent and talk to him. You'll try talking with the other tenants in the building where Jillian lives. We might as well take the Underground. It's easier than finding a parking spot and can be quicker than driving."

Joe shifted in his chair for a moment. At last he finally burst out, "You know, I'm really more of a show-biz expert than you are."

Frank gave his brother a look. "Joe, this Ian Fisher-Stone doesn't sound like a big talent agent. I don't think he'll have a bunch of hot-looking girls hanging around his waiting room."

"Do you think I'd be distracted from my duties by a bunch of beautiful actresses?"

"Yes, I do." Frank picked up the check, pulled some bills from his pocket, and gave them to the silent waiter who'd materialized beside them.

Joe sighed as he pushed back from the table.

"I hate to admit it, Frank, but you're probably right."

The dirty brick building on the edge of Soho was narrow and tired-looking. The tiles in the entrance were all cracked, and so was the glass on the building directory. A shadowy stairway led up to Ian Fisher-Stone's third-floor office. It smelled of stale cigar smoke.

As Frank climbed past the tattoo parlor on the second floor he began to suspect that Jillian's agent wasn't high on the ladder of success. The dingy, tiny reception room he finally reached seemed to confirm that. Holes actually showed through the worn Oriental carpet, and the photos on the walls were faded from age. Piled high on a small reception desk were dozens of fat, dusty file folders.

Since there was no one seated behind the cluttered desk, Frank crossed the threadbare rug and tapped on the frosted glass door. Peeling gold letters spelled out *Ian Fisher-Stone, Talent Representatives*.

When Frank rattled the door, a muffled voice said something unintelligible.

Frank turned the dented brass doorknob.

The agent's inner office was no larger than the outer one. His desk was about the same size and equally cluttered. There were more piles of crammed folders leaning on a row of battered wooden filing cabinets along one wall. The framed photos of actors and actresses on these walls weren't quite as old and faded as the ones outside. Frank noticed a gap in the lowest row. Unfaded wallpaper showed where a photo had been.

Fisher-Stone himself was something of a surprise. He was a heavy, red-faced man with slicked-down blond hair and a mustache, quite dapper in a tweedy suit and a silk ascot tie. "Yes, my lad, how can I be of service?" he asked, motioning Frank to a rickety chair facing his desk.

"My name is Frank Hardy," Frank said as he sat. "My brother and I want to locate one of your clients."

The agent said, "You look quite young—if you don't mind my saying so—to be a 'tec.' "

Frank shrugged. "But we are investigators. And we're looking for Jillian Seabright."

"Our Jill, eh? Very fine girl." Fisher-Stone pronounced the word more like "gell."

Frank continued. "Do you have any idea where she might be?"

Fisher-Stone made a vague fluttering gesture with one hand. "Over the hills and far away," he answered, chuckling. "She's off on some holiday jaunt. Not sure exactly where, old boy."

"She simply dropped out of the play she was in?"

"Opportunity, don't you know, for an unexpected bit of vacation. Off she went."

"And this doesn't bother you?"

"Not a bit," answered the agent. "Well, no, I take that back. There has been a good deal of interest in our Jill the past week or so. Inquiries from movie companies and the like. Most inconvenient, not being able to say where she went."

"Movie offers?"

"Ah, yes. Her career seems on the brink of taking off, I'd say. Imagine those blokes have seen her in"—for a second Fisher-Stone's eyes went vague—"that play of hers."

Frank gave the man a sharp glance. "I keep forgetting the title. What is that play?"

Fisher-Stone flipped a fingertip along his mustache. "Truth to tell, dear boy, I can never remember it myself. Fine play, though, and Jill is splendid in it."

Frank nodded. "I've heard that she's especially good in the hospital scene."

"Yes, she got raves for that."

Frank said, "A photograph of her would be very helpful."

"Sorry, my lad, don't have a one left."

"How's that?"

"Well, with all this increased interest in our Jill, I've been sending a lot of them around." He gestured at the gap in the line of wall photos. "Even had to ship off my own autographed pic of the child."

"How about negatives?"

The agent fluffed his mustache again. "Off at

a photography shop. Pop by toward the end of next week and I'll have a likeness of Jill that I'll be happy to turn over to you."

He stood up, straightening his ascot. "Frightfully sorry, but I have an important meeting with the BBC very shortly. I'll have to ask you to run along."

Rising from his chair, Frank stepped over to the filing cabinets. "Why don't I just check Jillian's file—just to make sure there aren't any photos left." He found a drawer marked P–S and reached for the handle.

"Not too likely." The agent came swiftly out from behind his desk, whipping a wicked-looking blackjack from inside his expensive jacket.

Frank dodged the first swing and aimed a solid punch at the older man's ribs.

But Fisher-Stone showed he had some quick moves. He twisted, and Frank's knuckles only scraped along the man's side. The blackjack flashed, catching Frank at the elbow. His arm went numb.

He tried a chop with his other hand, but the man brought the blackjack up against the side of Frank's head.

Frank staggered back and was hit twice more, hard. He dropped to the floor, the man's voice ringing in his ears.

"You're much too curious, my lad. Too curious for your own good."

Chapter
5

JILLIAN SEABRIGHT'S APARTMENT was on the
third floor of a gray stone building in a mews
just a few blocks from Baker Street. The building was managed by a heavyset woman in her
late sixties. She wore a long, heavy sweater over
a flower-patterned dress. Her hair had been dyed
a reddish shade of blond.

"I've been wondering somewhat about the
poor dear myself," she confided to Joe after
he'd explained that he was trying to find Jillian.
"Come in, and I'll fix you a cup of tea."

Grinning, Joe followed her into the building
and along a shadowy hall to her ground-floor
flat. "Do you remember the last time you saw
Jillian?"

"Well, now, it was . . . let me see." The

36

woman shuffled into her parlor on slippered feet, nodding him toward a yellow chintz armchair. "Must be a good ten days. It was that night we had such a fearful rainstorm."

"I guess we weren't in London then." Joe sat as the woman disappeared into the kitchen.

"I'll just put the water on," the woman said. "My name is Sharon Farnum—Mrs. Farnum, though I've been a widow nearly eight years now."

Returning to the parlor, she settled into a chair opposite Joe. "Is it some sort of trouble poor Jillian's in?"

"Someone is anxious to talk to her about some movie work."

"She's a very talented actress, is Jillian. I saw her in that play—'Tis a Pity She Won't Be Woo'd. Very good she was, although I didn't understand a word of the play itself."

"Could you tell me more about the last time you saw her?"

"It was a weeknight, about ten days ago, as best I can recall." Mrs. Farnum frowned, trying to drag up some memories. "She was on her way to the theater for that evening's performance. I'd just been marketing and saw her coming downstairs. She lives up on the third floor."

"Did you talk to her?"

"Just a bit of a chat—reminding her to take an umbrella—and she was off."

Joe frowned. "You haven't seen her since?"

The teakettle started to whistle. Mrs. Farnum shook her head and rose, and Joe followed her to the kitchen doorway. "Jillian didn't give you any notice that she was going away?"

"She didn't, no. Though at first I wasn't too concerned. I mean, her rent's paid for the month, and her things are still in her flat." Mrs. Farnum poured the boiling water into a blue teapot.

"Does she go away often?"

"Now and then, mostly to do a play out in one of the provincial theaters."

"Does she usually tell you when she expects to be gone for a while?"

Settling the teapot, two blue cups, and a bowl of sugar on a tray, Mrs. Farnum carried it back into the parlor. "Jillian always told me where she was off to and how long she'd be gone. She's a very considerate girl." She frowned. "That's why, I must admit, I've been a little concerned this time. It isn't like her to be gone so long without leaving word."

"Over the past few weeks, ma'am, has she had any unusual visitors?"

"Not that I—wait, I'm a liar. One night about two weeks ago I happened to stay up late to catch a special program on the telly. I noticed a very fancy car dropping Jillian off. Quite grand, it was—a Rolls-Royce."

"Did you get a glimpse of the driver?"

"That I didn't, Mr. Hardy." She shook her head. "Milk for your tea?"

"No thanks, ma'am," he said. "Did Jillian have any regular boyfriends?"

"Not recently, no."

"Any old boyfriends who might have made trouble for her sometime or another?"

Mrs. Farnum froze over her cup in mid-pour. "You suspect the child's come to grief, don't you?"

"We don't have any idea yet what's become of her," Joe said. "But when people disappear, it helps to know if anybody's been making threats."

"Oh, that's terrible." The teapot rattled against the cup as Mrs. Farnum's hand shook. She nervously bit at her lower lip. "Poor Jillian."

"We don't know anything yet. She may be perfectly fine someplace. Don't get upset."

Mrs. Farnum resumed pouring. "Did that person in that fancy car do her harm?"

"I don't know, but I'm curious about who might have been driving it."

She rose and handed him a cup of tea. "Help yourself to sugar."

"I'll drink it straight," he replied. "What about the other tenants here—how many are there?"

"At the moment there's just Miss Lore and Mr. Singh."

"Are they at home?"

"Miss Lore is over in Paris on business. Mr. Singh—a very nice young man from India—is at the bank where he works."

After taking a sip of his tea, Joe put the cup on a small table near his chair. "I'd like to have a look around Jillian's rooms."

"Well now, I don't know . . ."

"She might have left something behind—something that would help us find her."

"Yes, I can see where that's possible," Mrs. Farnum said. "Tell you what. I'll give you my passkey, and you can just trot up for a look. I'm expecting a phone call from my cousin Irene. I'm afraid I'll just have to wait here."

She pressed the key into Joe's hand. "Take your look around, then pop in here and return the key. And do tell me if you find anything."

"I will, ma'am."

"You sure you don't mind my not coming along with you?"

Joe smiled. "Not at all," he assured her.

The apartment was at the rear of the building on the top floor. A large, slanting skylight in the living room let in gray midmorning light. Rain spattered on the glass panes in a steady rhythm.

Joe went quickly through the whole place first, checking out each room and making sure the young woman wasn't there. He looked into all the closets, even under the bed. Jillian—or

40

worse, her dead body—wasn't there. The flat was very neat and tidy. After searching, he noted that he didn't see a single photo of the missing young woman.

"I don't think I've ever seen or heard of an actress who didn't keep pictures of herself around," Joe muttered as he passed from the kitchen to the living room, glancing around.

The antique trunk that served as a coffee table was bare. And although there were spaces on the bookshelves for little glass vases and knick-knacks, there were no pictures frames.

Beyond the living room, Joe found a neatly made bed and a bedroom in perfect order. There was no sign of a struggle having taken place. He looked again into the clothes closet, which gave off a faint scent of flowery perfume.

Joe noticed that there was probably a suitcase missing. A set of matching luggage sat in a row on the closet floor. There was a gap between suitcases two and three—a space large enough to hold another suitcase. Fallen across the largest bag was an expensive-looking black evening dress. Not something a girl would leave lying, wrinkled, on the floor of her closet, he thought.

Joe frowned. Suppose it was a rush job—somebody grabbing clothes to toss into that missing suitcase so it would look as if Jillian had packed her bag. They wouldn't care about a wrinkled dress that had fallen off its hanger.

On the other hand, maybe Jillian was just sloppy. Joe shook his head. That didn't fit in with how neat she'd left the room—the whole apartment, in fact.

Joe checked the bureau drawers, the boxes on the top shelves of the closet, and under the bed—twice. But he turned up no pictures at all. None of Jillian, none of Jed Shannon, none of anyone. No letters, either.

He had the feeling that someone had been through the girl's flat fairly recently and done some careful editing of its contents.

In the living room, Joe did find something, but he wasn't sure what it meant.

Beside the trunk he found a small pile of magazines. Five of them were fashion or theater periodicals, all with recent dates. But the sixth was a British newsweekly that had come out five months earlier. Joe found a small red paper clip serving as a page marker. Opening the magazine, Joe found a piece about a young woman named Emily Cornwall.

According to the story, Miss Cornwall was the heiress to not one but two large fortunes and had been living abroad for several years in a warmer climate because of her health. Rumors had reached the magazine that the heiress would be returning to England in a few months. Under the will of her late, eccentric grandfather, Sir Danvers Talbot, she was due to receive "the fabled Talbot emeralds" on her twenty-first birthday. That date would fall—

Joe glanced at the date on his watch. Just three days from today.

He examined a grainy black-and-white photograph, shot from a distance with a telephoto lens. It showed a slim young woman sitting on a sunlit patio next to a plump older woman. Emily Cornwall seemed pretty but looked frail.

Joe spread the magazine on Jillian's desk while he searched it. Every cubbyhole was empty. There wasn't even an unpaid bill to be found.

His back was to the flat's front door when he heard it swing open.

Then he heard a voice say evenly, "I have a gun. Just stay right where you are."

Chapter

6

JOE LOOKED OVER his shoulder, stared, then turned around to face the intruder. "Still looking for your lost dog, Red?"

Standing in the open doorway was the red-haired young woman he'd bumped into after last night's shooting. She still had her black shoulder bag, but this time she had her hand thrust inside it.

"My hair is auburn, not red. What are you doing here?"

"Funny, I was about to ask you the same question."

The young woman came into the living room, pushing the door closed with one leg. "I'm looking for Jillian Seabright."

"So am I. That could mean we're on the same side of whatever game's being played."

A thoughtful look came into the woman's eyes. "Who are you?"

"Joe Hardy. Sorry I didn't get around to introducing myself last night. And you?"

"You wouldn't have a brother named Frank, would you?"

Joe sighed. "Sometimes I wish I had a choice in that matter. But I have to admit I do."

"The Hardy brothers. You're sort of detectives."

"Sort of," Joe repeated, grinning. "And your name is . . . ?"

"Oh, I'm Karen Kirk." She pulled her right hand out of the bag, empty. "Really, I don't have a gun. But from the back you looked like you might be a burglar—or worse."

"Lots of people say that about me. You really are a friend of Jillian's?"

"Yes, I met her when I was in London last summer." Karen walked over to the sofa and sat down. "I interviewed her, in fact."

"You're a reporter?"

"Sort of." Karen grinned at him. "It was just an article on a promising young British actress for my high school paper back in Connecticut." Her grin faded. "This trip, though, I'm working for *Teen Travel* magazine in New York. It's a summer intern program, and I was supposed to stay with Jillian for the two weeks I'm in London."

"When did you arrive?"

"Two days ago. I came right here, but she wasn't around. I checked into a youth hostel, and I've been trying to find her ever since."

"How did you get in today?"

"I finally managed to track down an actress friend of hers who had a spare key to the flat. But she didn't know where Jillian had gone." Karen shrugged. "Anyway, I came here today just to look around her flat. Hoping, you know, to find some clue as to where she is. Do you think she's in trouble, or in some kind of danger?"

Joe straddled the desk chair. "First tell me what you were doing hanging around Jed Shannon's place last night."

"I knew Jillian was planning to see him when he came to London," she answered. "I was intending to ask if he had any idea where I could find her."

"How did you get his address?"

"Oh, I know some people working for one of the teen magazines over here. It wasn't too tough to get his temporary address."

"It wasn't tough for whoever pumped a couple of shots at us, either." Joe got up, remembering something, and headed for the phone table next to the sofa. "Why didn't you go ahead and try to talk to Jed?"

"I was right across the street when that man shot at you." Karen shook her head. "It suddenly didn't seem like such a safe place to be. I decided I wouldn't want anyone linking me up with Jed Shannon. So I ran and hid—and then I met you."

Joe raised his eyebrows. "You mean there isn't any Bozo?"

Karen sighed. "I made up the dog."

"What kind was he?"

She thought about it. "A Great Dane, probably."

"Did you get a look at the guy who shot at us?" Joe picked up the phone receiver and began unscrewing the mouthpiece. "Keep talking."

"Do you expect to find a bug?"

"I want to check it out. Tell me about the guy."

"Well, he was crouching down behind a car almost directly across from Jed's house. I was about half a block away on the same side of the street. But because of the fog, I didn't see the man till he popped up and took two shots at you. Then he took off, and so did I—in the opposite direction."

"So it was you I saw running off." Joe gave Karen a piercing look. "Can you describe him?"

"Big, wide shoulders, wearing a pea coat— like sailors in the movies. A knit cap—dark clothes. I didn't get a good look at his face, but I think maybe he had a broken nose."

THE HARDY BOYS CASEFILES

"Young?"

"Not especially—maybe in his thirties."

Joe frowned in thought. Could have been the one who left us a note, he said to himself. He cut Karen off before she could bombard him with questions. "Somebody planted a threat in our car."

"Sounds like you should have locked the door."

"It *was* locked." Joe dug a small electronic listening device out of the phone and dropped it on the table. "This is how they knew about Jed Shannon." He picked up a heavy ashtray and smashed the bug.

Karen stared at the pieces as if they hid a great mystery. "This doesn't make any sense to me, Joe. Bugs in the phone, mysterious gunmen. It's like something out of a spy novel."

"More like someone with a very efficient staff is interested in Jillian."

"You didn't answer my question before. Is she in danger?"

"I'd say she is. But nobody's been killed so far."

"You don't know that for certain." Karen's voice rose. "Jillian might be dead right now."

"I don't think so." Joe responded. "The bad guys—whoever they may be—are working too hard to keep us from looking for her."

"That doesn't mean she's not dead."

"Forgive my being blunt, but if she were

48

dead, she couldn't tell us anything about her captors. So the fact that people are trying to stop us is a good sign." Joe picked up the news magazine, which he'd left on the desk. "Does this mean anything to you?"

Karen studied the marked story. "Not much, I'm afraid. As far as I know, Jillian didn't know this Emily Cornwall." She started to hand the magazine back, then stopped. "But there is one thing."

"What?"

"Well, this girl in the picture—Emily Cornwall, I mean. She does look incredibly like Jillian. Of course, she's a brunette, and Jillian's blond. And she doesn't look anywhere near as healthy as Jillian, but the resemblance is amazing."

"When's the last time you and Jillian talked?"

"Two weeks ago. I phoned to confirm the details of my visit."

Taking the magazine back, Joe folded it under his arm. "Did she mention a big movie role that was coming her way, or maybe a nice part in a new play?"

Frowning, Karen answered, "Yes, she did. She wasn't full of details, though. All she said was that there was a good possibility she'd soon be as rich as I was."

"You're rich?"

"Not me, actually, no." Karen looked down

at her hands. "But my father happens to be a millionaire."

"That's a nice sort of father to have. How was Jillian planning to get rich?"

"It was from an acting job. But, as I say, she was reluctant to talk about it."

Joe gave Karen a skeptical look. So Jillian had a big acting job coming up—that seemed like a pretty poor time to disappear on a vacation. "Was she usually that closemouthed?" he asked.

"No, not Jillian. This time, however, I had the impression someone had cautioned her not to talk about this particular job. Show business people can be very secretive at times—'Don't tell anyone about this, or it might spoil the deal.'"

Joe shook his head. This whole situation made no sense. Threats against Jed, warnings not to look for Jillian. Jillian's disappearance—which might or might not be wrapped up with a secret acting job. Karen Kirk's appearance on the scene right after her friend disappeared. And where did the magazine article in his pocket fit in? There were altogether too many questions here, and far too few answers.

He checked his wristwatch. "I'm due to meet Frank for lunch in half an hour," he said. "If you came along, we could pool what we know."

"Are you inviting me to lunch?"

"Yeah, in a purely businesslike way, understand," Joe said with a wide grin.

A quick ride on the London Underground brought them to the Bloomsbury area and the restaurant where Joe was supposed to meet Frank. A huge sign in the window read Real American-style Burgers. They grabbed a white Formica-topped table and settled in to wait for Frank. After fifteen minutes, Joe went ahead and ordered sodas and burgers for Karen and himself.

They took nearly half an hour to arrive. And after one bite, Joe stared at the shriveled-up beef patty in his bun. "American burgers, huh?" He glanced at Karen. "Does this taste like a Connecticut burger to you? It sure doesn't taste like a Bayport burger."

Karen put her bun down, too, giving Joe a lopsided smile. "Maybe it fools the British, but not two hungry Americans."

"Right now I'm more worried about lost Americans." Joe looked at his watch, frowning. "Frank should have been here when we arrived. Now he's almost forty-five minutes late."

He dug some money out of his pocket to pay for the almost-untouched burgers.

"Something's wrong here, very wrong. I think Frank's in trouble—and I know the first place to check."

Chapter

7

THE WORLD WAS FADED, woolly, and full of dust. At least, that's how it seemed to Frank Hardy as he came to. He sneezed on the dust and regretted it. Sneezing isn't smart when you're dizzy, sick, and have an awful headache.

Frank was just getting his face out of the old carpet when he heard footsteps approaching. He struggled to his feet.

Ian Fisher-Stone—or whoever it was—wasn't going to get away with it a second time. Catching a blurry glimpse of legs, Frank lunged into a tackle.

"Hey!" a voice burst out.

"Nice play, Frank," said another voice.

Frank was down on the rug again, where he

discovered he'd just tackled a young woman wearing jeans.

His brother, Joe, stood just beyond the tangle, grinning. He helped Karen up and said to Frank, "Glad to see you're conscious. Let me introduce you to Karen Kirk."

"Sorry about that," muttered Frank as Karen helped him up.

Karen looked at Frank and said, "That's okay. I'm getting used to being jumped by men I've never seen before. You take after your brother in that respect." Then she asked, "What happened? When you didn't show up for lunch, your brother and I hurried over here. Why were you on the floor?"

Frank touched his head carefully. "I was dumb," he answered. "So I got rapped on the skull because of it."

"By Fisher-Stone?" Joe asked.

"By a guy who *wasn't* Fisher-Stone but tried to convince me he was."

Joe looked carefully at his brother. "You'd better see a doctor. Maybe at the hotel . . ."

"I'll be okay."

"You could have a concussion," said Karen.

"I've been hit on the head before, and this doesn't feel like a . . . Hey, what's that?"

Lying on the rug where he'd been sprawled was a crumpled piece of paper. "Looks like a railroad timetable—whoa!" Bending to pick up the paper, Frank suddenly felt woozy.

Joe caught his wobbly brother and guided him to a chair. "Even if you don't have a concussion, sit down for a while."

Karen gathered up the fallen timetable, straightened it out, and leafed through it. "This might mean something." She pointed to one of the station names—circled in pencil.

Joe squinted. "Whoever bopped you noted down the train departure times for Beswick."

"That's down in Kent, I think. About a hundred miles from London," Karen said.

"Beswick . . . Beswick," murmured Joe. He snapped his fingers, grinned, and tugged out the news magazine he'd slipped into his back pocket. "That's the town where Emily Cornwall is supposed to go— No, by now she's living there, at the Talbot estate."

"Maybe I'm groggier than I realized." Frank gave him a look. "I don't seem to know what the heck either of you is talking about. And who *is* this Karen Kirk?"

"Oh, she's the redhead—um, the auburn-haired young woman I met last night," Joe said. "You know, the one who was walking a dog—except there was no dog."

"Oh, sure, that's clear so far."

"I'm a friend of Jillian Seabright's," Karen told him. "I'm looking for her, too."

"Karen's a reporter from Connecticut. She was supposed to room with Jillian while she's over here on vacation."

Frank rubbed his forehead. "How long was I out? You learned her entire life story, and—"

"A good investigator asks the right questions," Joe told him. "You can get a lot of information quickly that way."

"Fine—so now suppose you tell me who Emily Cornwall is. And why Beswick is suddenly the hottest town in England."

"Read." Joe set the open magazine on the edge of the cluttered desk. "That's Emily Cornwall in the picture—the thin one."

"I can read the caption." Frank glared at his brother. "So?"

"If you bothered to *keep* reading . . ." Joe said, pointing at another paragraph in the story. "See here? Emeralds. Heiress. Emily Cornwall seldom seen. Returns to England."

"And?"

"We found the magazine, with that particular story marked, in Jillian's apartment," Karen said. "This Emily Cornwall person looks quite a lot like Jillian."

Joe looked at Frank. "Does that fact suggest to you what it suggests to me?"

"It's a possibility," Frank said.

"Let's cut the mumbo-jumbo," Karen said. "You think Jillian may be impersonating Emily Cornwall?"

"I think it's worth looking into," Frank said.

"There's the big money Jillian was hoping to

make," Joe pointed out. "But I'm not sure where the man in the Rolls-Royce fits in."

Frank rolled his eyes. "What man in the Rolls-Royce?"

Joe ran through what he'd learned from Mrs. Farnum. "So that's the whole story. Whatever's up doesn't sound very legal."

Karen cut in. "I know Jillian—she'd never do anything that was against the law."

"This Emily Cornwall business is just one possibility." Frank frowned. "It might even be some kind of curve ball to throw us off—pitched by the people who kidnapped Jillian." His frown deepened. "If, of course, she was actually kidnapped."

"I think that knock you took has put all sorts of weird ideas in your head," Joe said. "Maybe you should take the afternoon off."

"No, I can handle it. Besides, we have an appointment at the theater this afternoon." Frank tested his sore head again and winced. "There's a matinee of *'Tis a Pity She Won't Be Woo'd,* and we'll be able to talk to most of the people who worked with Jillian."

Karen picked up the news magazine. "Let me show this to some friends in the magazine biz. I won't give away anything, and I may be able to find out more about Miss Cornwall and her fortune."

"Sounds like a good idea," Joe said. "Then

you and I can meet for dinner afterward, Karen, to talk over what you've found out.''

Frank took his brother aside. "Joe, you and I are supposed to be handling this case. We don't need volunteer help.''

"I do," Joe told him, and then turned back to Karen. "Dig into Emily Cornwall—as a personal favor to me.''

Karen smiled and dropped the magazine into her big black shoulder bag. She turned to Frank. "I really am a good reporter," she said. "I'll get you all the information there is to be found.''

Frank studied her silently for a few seconds. "Okay," he said finally. "We'll see.''

The manager of the Piccadilly Rep, the company presenting *'Tis a Pity She Won't Be Woo'd,* was putting on his makeup for the play. "I'm flattered that an American movie agent— Larry Berman—was interested in our show.''

The man glued pieces of bushy black beard to his face, having painted his nose and cheeks bright red. "I play Sir Toby Bearpit," he said, talking to Frank's and Joe's reflections in his makeup mirror. "Even gotten some excellent notices. 'Ralph Estling is more than adequate.' That's from the London *Times*, my boys.''

"I'm happy for your career," Frank told him. "But I'm afraid Larry Berman didn't arrange this meeting to check out your play. We're trying to locate Jillian Seabright. Why did she quit?"

"According to her agent, she got a better offer." Estling puffed out his cheeks, snarling so his white teeth showed under the false hair. "Beard is just about right, I think."

"We're talking about Ian Fisher-Stone here?" Frank asked.

"Yes, old Ian. Not much of an agent, as I told Jilly many a time. She's a very talented lady and deserves much better representation."

"You've met Fisher-Stone?"

"Yes, unfortunately. I'm not partial to having whiskey fumes breathed on me."

Frank nodded to his brother. "How did he let you know Jillian was leaving—in person?"

"No, thank heaven, merely over the telephone. 'Dear gell is off to do a major role, old man.' Something like that."

Joe said, "And you just let Jillian out of her contract with you?"

Estling smiled, still carefully smoothing his beard. "We're a pretty informal lot—don't pay much, either. So if Jilly had a chance to do better for herself, I wouldn't stand in her way."

"Did Jillian ever discuss this big part with you?" Frank asked.

"Never said a word, but that's not unusual." Estling put on a wild black wig, then slipped into a padded coat. Joe stared. He'd watched the actor transform himself from a burly but mild-mannered type to a rather scary-looking bully.

"When did the agent call you?" Joe asked. "Before or after her final performance?"

"Morning after." Estling's voice became a booming growl as he started getting into character. "Good thing we had an understudy. She's not quite as good as Jilly was, but more than adequate. Well, my lads, I'm in the first scene, and the curtain's going up very soon. Any more questions?"

"Not now," said Frank, grinning at the transformation. "But we'd like to talk to some of the other people in the company who knew Jillian."

"I'll allow that. Just don't make anyone miss his or her cue." Estling gave a final fluff to his false beard, made a low rumbling sound in his chest, and strode to the dressing room door, grandly yanking it open. "If you run into Jilly, give her my best."

The Hardys split up, Frank hitting the dressing rooms while Joe checked the green room, where the actors congregated between scenes.

After knocking on two doors and getting no answer, Frank heard a reply at the third. A high, fluting voice said, "Come in."

A plump sixty-year-old actress introduced herself as Beatrix Graill. And from the look of things, she didn't intend to leave her dressing room for a while.

"We have plenty of time for your questions,

young man," she told him as she heated water for tea on a hot plate. "Lady Victoria Gadabout doesn't make her entrance until the second act."

"You knew Jillian well?"

"We were friends, yes. I'll explain why I'm so interested in talking to you—in addition to concern for the girl, that is." The actress sat down, carefully shifting her wide skirt with its rustling petticoats. "Two years ago I played Mrs. Dillingham on television."

Frank nodded. "That's right, the lady detective. I thought you looked familiar. We saw that on a public broadcasting station in America."

"The old girl's dottier and frowzier than I am." Frank noted that she looked a lot different now, in an elaborately curled and powdered wig. "Playing a detective got me interested in investigating. I read lots of mysteries—you might call me an amateur sleuth." She grinned. "Or an annoying busybody. Jillian probably would describe me the second way."

"Was there some reason—"

"Yes—and its name is Nigel Hawkins." Beatrix Graill deftly poured boiling water from a saucepan into a cracked china teapot.

"You sound like you're describing some kind of awful insect."

"Rather close," she answered. "The acting profession, alas, has many a shady person on its fringes. Nigel is one of the shadiest. It pained me to see Jillian dining with him at one of my favorite Soho restaurants a few weeks ago."

"What does this Hawkins do?"

"He's a producer of low-budget films, at the rate of about one every other year or so. Dismal things, designed to cash in on some current fad—punk music, celebrity lawsuits, political scandals. Although Nigel seemingly makes a good living, none of his movies ever pays off for the investors. Or for the poor actresses and actors—and they certainly don't help their careers."

"Was Jillian planning to be in one of Hawkins's films?"

"I certainly hope not," Ms. Graill said. "The fact that she departed so suddenly, however, makes me worry. Maybe she did agree to work for that dreadful man."

"But Jillian didn't actually tell you she'd signed up with him?"

"She acted very odd when I mentioned that I'd seen them together." The plump actress suddenly dug a hand into an open trunk nearby. "Ah, look at this." She held up a framed photo. "Nigel in the flesh. He's the handsome chap at the left of this garden party group, just next to me."

Frank took the picture and studied it. Nigel Hawkins was a tall, thin man of about fifty. Very well dressed, his light hair worn long and wavy, his small mustache neatly clipped. "Does he have an office in London?"

"Last time I heard. A small one, in an unfashionable part of the city."

"Perhaps I should go talk to him."

Beatrix Graill returned to her teapot. "Be on your guard with that man," she warned. "I've heard rumors that he's been in more things than questionable films. This is all hearsay, mind you. But there's been talk that he's involved in fencing stolen gems."

"So he'd be interested in, say, emeralds."

"Just about anything that sparkles."

A heavy fist knocked on the door. When Beatrix opened the door, Joe came bursting into the dressing room. "Trouble," he announced.

"What's happened?" Frank asked.

"Larry Berman called us here at the theater—he remembered the appointment he'd set up." Joe looked a little numb. "He wanted to know if Jed was with us. When I told him he wasn't, Berman got really upset."

Frank took a deep breath. "Are you saying what I think you're saying?"

Joe nodded unhappily. "Looks like Jed Shannon has disappeared, too."

Chapter

8

FRANK AND JOE took a taxi to Jed's town house, where they met up with Larry Berman, wearing a different, even more explosive Hawaiian shirt this afternoon. "I'm worried, guys, really worried. My boy may be in danger—and on top of that, we blew six interviews." From the amount of pacing going on in the town house living room lately, Joe wondered if there'd be any rug left.

"Give us some details," Frank told the nervous agent.

"The day was going beautifully," Berman began. "Jed's a bright boy, and the media people love him. He's very good at interviews and can be, you know, likable, funny, sincere—whatever the situation calls for.

"Okay, so we're at *London Stitches,* a very trendy fashion magazine. In the middle of the interview a girl walks into the editorial offices to say there's an important call for Jed. I'm about to tell her to get lost, but he jumps up and goes out to take it in the reception area."

"So who was the call from?" Joe asked.

"Jed never told me. When he came back to continue the interview, I asked him who was on the horn. He said it was nothing important." The agent shrugged. "After that we stopped for coffee at some dinky overpriced bistro. Jed said he had to use the washroom. And stupidly, I let him go alone."

Berman shook his head. "After about ten minutes, I sent those bonehead security guys who were with us out hunting for him. He was nowhere to be found. But they dug up a waiter who told me he saw Jed head out the back door."

"Alone?" Frank asked.

"From what the waiter told me, yes."

Frank shook his head. "Then it doesn't look as though Jed was kidnapped."

"Maybe they lured him outside somehow and grabbed him there." Berman did some more unhappy pacing. "Anyway, I haven't heard from him since, and we're talking *hours* here. I'm in a major bind."

Frank stared. He'd never seen someone actually wring his hands before.

Berman stopped wringing and mopped his fore-head. "Do you have any idea what Jed is worth to my agency? If any suspicion got back to my bosses that I've let him just disappear . . ."

His voice died out. "I'll be finished in Holly-wood. Nobody will trust me—*nobody*."

"You'd better go to the police again," Joe suggested.

"No *way* I can do that." The agent shook his head vigorously. "What if Jed just sneaked away to meet some lady? I mean, he's been known to do that now and then. To avoid any kind of bad publicity, we've got to find him quietly. Can you help me out here?"

Frank frowned in thought. "I'd say the most likely explanation for Jed's action is that he got some kind of news about Jillian Seabright."

"Do you have the phone number for *London Stitches?*" Joe asked.

From the pocket of his loud shirt Berman took out a wad of memo slips. "Yeah. Here it is." He plucked out a slip of paper and handed it over.

Picking up the nearest phone, Joe called the magazine. "I'm a member of Mr. Jed Shannon's staff, and I've got a problem," he said into the receiver. "Mr. Shannon received a telephone message while he was at your offices earlier. He was supposed to take some notes—and lost them."

Joe worked very hard to make his voice sound

sincere. "Worst of all, he doesn't remember the caller's name. So if—oh, you're the one who took the call. Do you remember the name—Dickens? Bert Dickens? Great. Thanks a million." Putting the phone down, he glanced over at Berman.

"Means nothing to me." The agent gave them a baffled shrug.

Frank was already digging out the telephone directory. "Here it is. Bert Dickens—and he lists himself as a private inquiry agent."

Joe had a grim smile on his face. "Looks like Jed didn't think we were good enough for this job." He looked hard at Berman. "Did he hire himself another detective?"

"If he did, he sure didn't tell me about it. But Jed's been very upset about this Jillian. And he did mention that he thought you were a little young."

"He's not that much older than we are himself," Joe pointed out.

"Acting and detecting are two different things," Berman said.

Joe gestured to the phone book, still in his brother's hand. "So do we give our friend Dickens a call?"

Frank shook his head. "I think this calls for a personal interview."

The address in the phone book was in East London. To get there from Jed Shannon's town house, the easiest route was by way of the London Underground.

"Hey, Frank," Joe whispered after they'd gotten their tickets, "how far underground do these trains run?"

Two sets of escalators later they had finally reached the station platform. Frank thought the arriving train looked a little old-fashioned. It actually had a wooden floor. But it was surprisingly quiet—and very clean.

They switched trains after two stops, then rode on for what seemed like forever until they'd reached almost the other end of London.

Coming out of the station, they found themselves under gray skies in a quiet neighborhood of four-story brick buildings. Frank whipped out his pocket map of London and started off for the local main street.

"There—there it is," he said.

His brother, however, dug in his feet and began tugging on Frank's arm.

Frank gave him a look. "We don't have the time, Joe."

"I didn't have much lunch, since Karen and I cut it short to go hunting for you." He tried to look very sincere. "It seems to me, Frank, that fate is taking a hand. I mean, why else would this private eye have his office right over this fish-and-chips restaurant?"

They had stopped under the awning of the fast-food restaurant, the only dry spot on the rainy street. Joe was looking longingly through the window at the fried fish and french fries. Frank was trying to move him along.

"Let's go, Joe. This detective may know something about where Jed is."

"Okay, okay." Joe followed his brother to the stairway that led up to the second floor of the sooty old building. "I'll try to curb my hunger."

Frank decided that Bert Dickens wasn't enjoying much more success than Ian Fisher-Stone. The hand-lettered sign on the back of the index card held up with thumbtacks was an indication.

They headed up a steep stairway paneled with old, dark wood. It was also dimly lit and smelled strongly of stale oil from the fish-and-chips shop below.

"And yet another missing person," Joe remarked as they climbed upward.

"Jed may not be missing. It could be that he just decided to take off and look for Jillian on his own."

"I don't much like the idea of somebody we're trying to help sneaking off to get another detective behind our backs."

Frank shrugged. "He's impatient, and he's got lots of money. He probably figures the more detectives, the better. Sort of like doctors, when you get a second opinion."

They reached the second floor, opened a door, and entered a long hallway lined with office doors.

"This Nigel Hawkman you were telling me about, Frank. Do you think he—"

"Hawkins," corrected his brother. "If Larry Berman hadn't sent for us, Hawkins would have been the next person we'd have gone to see."

"The people we've questioned seem ready to swear that Jillian is honest," Joe said, frowning in thought. "But this whole business is beginning to sound like some kind of caper centering around the Cornwall girl and her emeralds."

"Here's Dickens's office." Frank nodded at a warped wooden door with a wrinkled business card tacked to it.

Joe took hold of the knob, pushing against the door. It opened inward about ten inches, then wouldn't budge. Leaning his weight into it, he got the door to open another two or three inches.

"Stuck?"

Joe poked his head through the opening. "Uh-oh. Come on, give me a hand here." He began pushing harder.

"What's blocking the door?" Frank demanded, adding his shoulder to the job of forcing an entrance.

"Just what we need," Joe answered. "A body."

Chapter

9

"HE'S BREATHING." After a brief struggle to move the door with the dead weight against it, Frank had squeaked his way through a bare sliver of doorway. Then he'd knelt down to the body lying on the floor. "I think this guy was just slugged—the same way I was."

The man he was examining lay on the hardwood floor of the small office. He was pudgy and middle-aged and had thinning reddish hair and a bushy mustache. And if anything, he had to be worse off than the seedy agent. His office didn't even have a rug.

"So this must be Bert Dickens, huh?" Joe helped his brother lift the unconscious man, carrying him over to an ancient leather couch against one wall.

As his head touched the cracked leather the man's eyes blinked. "Outsmarted me, they did," he announced in a slurred voice. "Made a total fool out of Bert Dickens."

"Take it easy," Frank cautioned. "You'd better lie still for a while, Mr. Dickens." He rubbed his own head. "I know how it feels."

Faded blue eyes took the Hardys in. "And who might you lads be?"

"I'm Frank Hardy, and this is my brother, Joe."

"My competition. Well, sir, I'll tell you—Bert Dickens would have been a lot better off if he'd let you two muck along in this mess on your own."

"You were working for Jed Shannon?"

Grunting, the middle-aged detective grabbed hold of Frank's arm and pulled himself to a sitting position on the swaybacked couch. "Been working for him these past two days," he said. "The lad hired me to find this missing sweetheart of his."

"Any luck?"

Dickens felt the lumps on his head, a pained expression on his face. "Doesn't look like it, now, does it?"

Frank did his best to keep a straight face. "I meant, do you have any idea of what's happened to Jillian Seabright?"

"Dead ends are all I've come up with."

Joe frowned. "But it was you who telephoned Jed Shannon this afternoon."

"That it was. This pair of blokes dropped in on me and, you might say, *persuaded* me to make that call."

"What did they look like?" Frank asked.

"The boss—at least he asked the questions and gave the orders—was a very natty chap. A round guy with a red face, blond, mustache, dressed like a gent."

"Sounds like the guy I met." Frank nodded. "He used a blackjack on me, too."

"No, it was the other bloke who got me," Dickens explained. "Big nasty boyo, he was, your typical thug. Maybe an ex-prizefighter, something like that. Looked like he'd been in a scrap or two in his lifetime."

"Let me guess," Joe said. "Did he have a broken nose?"

"That he did." Dickens rubbed his own face. "Thought he was going to take a crack at breaking mine."

"Maybe another old friend," Joe said. "The guy who took potshots at us the other night."

"They gave me a phone number to call," Dickens told them. "I was to say it was a real emergency to whoever answered—that I had to talk to Jed Shannon and nobody else. When he came on I was to tell him how I had important information about Jillian Seabright. I couldn't give it over the phone, and he was to rush right over here, not telling a soul.'' Dickens grimaced. ''Sounded to me as if the lad took the bait sure enough.''

''Did he come here?''

The detective started to shrug but decided it was too painful. ''I have no idea. Soon as I made that call, old Thuggo went to work. Must have done a proper job to leave me slumbering away on my own floor until now.''

Absorbing all the new information, Frank said, ''They seemed to know Jed's plans for the day, Joe, even though we got rid of the bugs on his phone.''

Joe nodded, turning to the detective. ''Is there anything we can do for you? Want us to call a doctor?''

''Not right yet. I'd just like to sit for a bit and collect what's left of my wits,'' Dickens said. ''You could do me one favor. Fetch that sign from my desk and hang it round the doorknob as you leave.''

The sign read Out to Lunch.

Joe obliged the detective, and he and Frank left the office.

Walking down the dimly lit staircase, Joe said, ''I'll bet they grabbed Jed as soon as he entered this building.''

''Now we have to find where they took him.'' Frank looked grim. ''Probably the same place they have Jillian.''

Joe grinned. "Try to see the bright side. At least we don't have to look for *two* places."

They stepped out of the building to find a new set of rain clouds washing the street.

"Still want those fish and chips, Joe?" Frank asked.

"Hard to pass up, but I'm intending to take Karen Kirk to dinner and see what she can tell me."

Joe and Frank headed for the Underground train. "I'll do a little digging on my own while you're with Karen," Frank proposed, "and catch up with you later. Where will I find you?"

"I thought we'd try Chumley's near the Strand," Joe said as they boarded the train. "You were the one who told me about it. You read about it in the guidebook. 'The historical restaurant on London's most historic street.' "

Back at the hotel, Joe grinned as his brother tossed him the car keys. "Do me a favor, okay? Don't come barging in on us until the end of the meal."

Chumley's restaurant consisted of three fairly large rooms. Thick oaken beams held up the ceilings, and the walls were paneled in dark wood. The windows were stained glass, and the waiters all wore tailcoats. Joe and Karen were seated at a small table in the innermost room. After the damp chill outside, the small fire crackling in the stone fireplace nearby felt welcome.

"Chumley's has been here for nearly two hundred years," Karen said, studying her menu.

"Wouldn't be surprised if our waiter has been, too." Joe was studying the pretty auburn-haired young woman sitting across from him.

Karen shut her menu and reached into her shoulder bag, which sat on the floor next to her chair. "I gathered some material for you," she said, taking out a large manila envelope and passing it to him.

Joe opened it to find a large photograph and two sheets of typed paper. "So, another picture of Emily Cornwall, huh?"

"Taken when she was eighteen. It's the only close-up shot of her anybody seems to have," Karen said. "A friend on one of the magazines made me a quick copy."

Joe frowned at the smiling face in the picture. "Now that you've seen this, do you still think she resembles Jillian?"

"They certainly are similar. If you dyed Jillian's blond hair to the same dark shade as Emily's, there'd be an amazing resemblance."

Slowly Joe placed the photo on the crisp white tablecloth. "Jillian Seabright disappears just as Emily Cornwall is about to return home and claim a very valuable necklace." He gazed up at the smoke-darkened beams in the ceiling. "Now, is that a coincidence? Or is somebody going to pull a switch—substitute Jillian for the heiress and collect the loot?"

"I'm telling you, Joe, Jillian would never willingly go along with anything like that."

"Suppose she's not willing? Maybe she's being forced to—Oh, sorry," Joe said to the waiter. "Give us a few more minutes to make up our minds, please."

Their aged, gray-haired waiter had silently appeared beside the table. "Very good, sir," the man said, and he withdrew.

"If it's a scam, we might have a line on the guy behind it," Joe said. "Does the name Nigel Hawkins ring any bells?"

Karen shook her head. "Jillian never mentioned him."

Joe started reading over the notes she'd given him. "They ought to fire whoever typed this. It has mistakes all over."

"I typed it."

Joe glanced over the top of the papers, his ears going red. "Then it's, uh, very creative. Um, especially the spelling."

"I'm not used to a manual typewriter anymore. At home I use a word processor. I took notes on everything in the files, then typed them up at the office on the only machine I could find." Karen's hands sat on the table, her fingers drumming it. "If it's not up to your high standards . . ."

"Hey, it's fine," Joe said. "I'm just used to noticing details." He grinned across at her. "So when I see Beswick spelled with a *z* and find

Emily with an *i* left out . . .'' Joe decided to change the subject. ''Well, I can make out that Emily Cornwall is definitely back in England.''

''She was severely injured in an auto accident three years ago in Paris,'' Karen said. ''She was lucky. Her parents were both killed.''

''That was right after she left school in Bern, Switzerland,'' Joe said, consulting the notes. ''Emily has been recuperating in Europe ever since. Nobody in England has seen her in years.''

''So it might not be impossible for an impostor to walk into the solicitor's office and claim the Talbot emeralds—which is just what Emily is supposed to do in three days.''

''Well, there's this companion to consider— what's her name?'' Joe went back to the papers. ''Right, Miss Sheridan. She's been with the family for six years, and with Emily every day since the accident.''

''Suppose someone bribed her?''

''Possible, but . . .'' Joe shook his head.

''How about this idea, then? The real Emily died in Europe.'' Karen leaned over the table, her hazel eyes sparkling with excitement. ''Miss Sheridan doesn't tell anybody, because that means her salary would stop. When it comes time to collect the emeralds, she decides to bring in a ringer.''

''We don't know enough about the companion, so all of this is just speculation,'' Joe said.

"There's also the problem of handwriting. Emily will obviously have to sign half a forest's worth of papers. You can't just stroll in and say, 'Hi, I look like Emily. Give me the gems.' "

"That's what you get for stopping after only the first page of my notes." Karen pointed to the top of the following page.

"Okay. Emily's right hand was broken in the car crash."

"So if I were going to impersonate her, I'd practice writing her signature. And if any of the lawyers said it didn't look quite right, I'd start crying a little. Then I'd remind them that I had to learn to write all over again after my awful accident."

"That might work," Joe agreed, "if she's right-handed."

"Next paragraph."

Joe read on. " 'Emily Cornwall is right-handed.' " He nodded. "Okay, it all seems to fall together. But we have to make sure we're not just jumping to conclusions. Jillian may have disappeared for entirely different reasons."

"May I make a suggestion?"

"Sure, what?"

"Let's order dinner," Karen said, "and not talk about any of this until we're finished."

They did exactly that. About two hours later they left Chumley's.

"What's your next move on this case?" Karen asked Joe.

He took her hand. "I want to talk it over with Frank," he said. "But I think a ride down to the village of Beswick would be a good idea."

Karen nodded. "I'll bet Jillian's down there, being kept against her will."

A fat raindrop splattered on the sidewalk next to them. More started falling in a sudden cloudburst. Joe glanced unhappily at the car, parked about two hundred feet away. "Maybe if we run . . ."

He set off, but Karen called, "Wait! I've got an umbrella in here somewhere."

Joe turned back to watch her start digging through her shoulder bag.

Behind him, the car exploded with a fiery roar.

Chapter

10

IT SEEMED to be raining fire and jagged chunks of metal as well as water.

Joe leapt for Karen, pulling her to the soggy sidewalk, shielding her body with his. The world seemed strangely silent after the blast.

"Are you okay?" Joe finally got his vocal cords to work.

"Y-yes," Karen managed. "Boy, you moved pretty fast. Did you get hurt?"

"Not as far as I can tell." Still on his knees, Joe glanced at the wreckage of the car. Flames were playing around it, and the rain sizzled on the hot metal. "Looks like the bad guys are really playing hardball now."

Suddenly he was on his feet, half-crouched. The

sound of running footsteps echoed in the fog. They could make out a blurred figure approaching.

"Everything all right?" Frank asked, skidding to a halt. He'd been heading toward the restaurant when the sound of the sudden explosion tore through the fog.

Joe helped Karen up. "Well, my hair feels like it's standing on end, and my ears are ringing worse than the last time we went to a rock concert. But outside of that, I don't think I have any problems."

Frank started back the way he came. "Then let's get away from here."

"Won't the police want to talk to you about your exploding automobile?" Karen asked.

"That's exactly why we have to make a getaway. We don't have anything solid to hand to the law right now. And we don't have time to waste, either."

Joe turned to Karen. "You up to some brisk hiking?"

She grinned. "Sure. All I seem to have is a few scrapes and bruises—and one ruined raincoat."

People with umbrellas were starting to appear, coming from restaurants and pubs. They surrounded the ruins of the car. Frank, Joe, and Karen turned their backs on the spectacle and slogged off in the rain.

"So where do we go from here?" Karen asked.

"I think it's time for a trip to beautiful Beswick," said Frank.

Joe grinned. "Just what I was about to suggest myself."

The three of them were able to catch the final train for Beswick that night. When they were settled into a compartment, Frank said, "What's the scoop, guys?"

From inside his coat Joe took the envelope Karen had given him. "Some background material on Emily Cornwall."

Studying the picture, Frank asked, "Does Jillian look like this?"

"Quite a bit," Karen admitted.

"So she could definitely impersonate the Cornwall girl." Frank turned his attention to the typewritten notes.

"But Jillian wouldn't do it—not just to make money," Karen said.

Joe chimed in with the theories that he and Karen had shared over the dinner table.

"There's a third possibility," Frank said, still reading. "Suppose Nigel Hawkins came to Jillian. She knows him as a movie producer. He tells her he's planning a film based on the life of an heiress like Emily. He auditions her, maybe gets her to pose for some photos in a dark wig."

"That would have worked." Karen, who was sharing a seat with Joe, suddenly hugged herself as if she'd gone cold. "I suppose Hawkins saw her someplace, in her play or on television, and realized how much she looked like Emily.''

"He could even have gotten her out of town without telling her what he really wanted her to do.'' Joe stared out at the fog-shrouded countryside rushing past. "He could have warned her not to tell anyone she was being considered for this big part.''

Frank set the pages and the picture on the seat beside him. "Which brings us to what I did tonight while you were feeding your faces,'' he said. "I paid a visit to Nigel Hawkins's offices. As I expected, he wasn't there. In fact, he hadn't been there for a while. The place was shut up tight.''

Joe sighed. "Another dead end.''

"Not exactly,'' Frank said. "I made a new friend—the concierge who takes care of the office building. He had a temporary forwarding address for Mr. Hawkins's mail—Beswick.''

Karen sat up straight. "Beswick—where Emily Cornwall is supposed to be staying.''

"Where Jillian Seabright may be,'' Joe added.

"*And* Jed Shannon,'' Karen said. "You know, if Hawkins had him, he could force Jillian to go through with that scam of his. Do the job or he'll hurt Jed.''

"That could work, sure,'' Frank conceded.

"Hawkins may have his troops at Beswick,'' Joe said.

"There's the dapper gent with the blackjack,

the guy with the broken nose—and probably lots of others who'll play rough." Frank frowned.

"The violence is getting worse and worse. We've gone from warning shots and threatening notes to beatings and car bombs." Joe's face was grim. "If the timing had been a little different, Karen and I would have been blown up tonight."

"I don't think so," his brother said.

"Hey, that car was totaled," Joe protested. "Anybody sitting in it—"

"That's my point, Joe. You *weren't* in it. These guys seem pretty efficient. They wouldn't set a bomb to go off at random, just hoping you'd be in the car at the time."

Karen leaned forward, resting her palm on her knee. "You're saying that the explosion was meant simply as another warning?"

"I'd guess that one of Hawkins's boys was watching. When he spotted you heading for the car, he detonated the bomb electronically from a safe distance."

"Risky," Joe objected. "They couldn't be sure that a fender wouldn't crack my skull—or the engine block wouldn't break Karen's neck."

"Ouch," she said, rubbing her neck.

"Oh, they're not saints, Joe. But they basically only wanted to scare us. If somebody got killed, well, that was too bad. But it wouldn't stop them from going ahead with their plans."

"Wait a second," Joe said. "To plant a bomb

in the car, they had to know where Karen and I were having dinner."

"I've been thinking about that." Frank was poker-faced. "They had to have somebody shadowing you."

"I usually spot tails."

"Well, you didn't this time—we'll all need to be especially careful."

Joe drummed the fingers of his left hand on the seat, looking again out of the window of the onrushing train.

After a few seconds of silence, Karen burst out, "There's another way they could have known. Why not mention it?"

"What?" Joe looked uncomfortable.

"I could have phoned them from the restaurant," she said. "After all, I did leave the table to visit the restroom."

"Hey," said Joe, "we all trust each other."

"Does Frank trust me?"

Frank met her stare. "Yes, Karen. I didn't bring up the possibility, because I *do* trust you. Okay?"

"I guess so."

After a few minutes of silence, Joe shifted in his seat. "Do they have a dining car on this train?"

"I'd think so," Karen said.

"Let's go find it. I need a soda—something to drink. We won't be in Beswick for nearly three hours, and nothing will be open by then."

"Not interested." Frank picked up the material on Emily Cornwall.

"Karen?"

"Not yet, Joe. After nearly getting blown up, I just want to sit back and take it easy."

"Well, I think I'll go foraging for supplies." Joe hesitated for a second in the doorway. "Can I bring anything back?"

Both Frank and Karen shook their heads.

"Then I'll see you in a while." Joe slid the door open and stepped into the corridor of the swaying train.

He'd gotten through two cars when his path was blocked by a little old lady carrying a covered basket. She was standing by a door that led out into the night in an otherwise empty stretch of corridor.

The train was passing through a less-settled section of countryside. The fog was thinning, but there wasn't much to see outside the glass window in the door. Joe saw only dark fields and an occasional distant light.

"Thank goodness!" The elderly woman's voice had a strange quavering tone as she called to Joe. "Could you help me, young man?"

"What's the problem, ma'am?"

"These silly spectacles. Could you hold my hamper for a moment?"

"Sure, I'd be glad to." Joe took the basket, which turned out to be unexpectedly heavy.

"Thank you so much." The woman removed

her rimless glasses and pulled a tissue from her pocket. She breathed on the lenses, bending over to do the job carefully. All Joe could see was wild gray hair peeking from beneath a patterned head scarf. Joe was amazed that such a frail-looking person could manage the heavy load she was toting. What did she have in there? Books? Bricks?

"That's much better." The woman slipped on her glasses and looked up at Joe with surprisingly young-looking eyes. She lifted the lid of the basket Joe was holding and yanked out a MAC-10 submachine gun.

Backing away, the old woman pointed the gun at Joe's chest. "Time for you to get off the train."

Joe stared. "But it's still moving."

The gun barrel poked him in the chest as his captor nodded. "That's exactly the idea."

Chapter
11

JOE STOOD FROZEN as the little old lady—who was, he realized a bit too late, actually a small man in disguise—opened the metal door. The machine gun poked Joe again in the ribs as the man said, "Had me worried there for a while. We had three drop-off points set up but passed two of them without a sight of you. Thought I'd have to do something right desperate to get one of you Hardys off alone. But third time lucky, I guess."

He glanced out the open doorway. "There'll be a car waiting for us. When we see a yellow lantern by the tracks, off we go."

"I don't think so, Granny." Joe dropped into a sudden crouch, swinging the hamper with all his strength.

The basket smashed into the gunman's hand, knocking the MAC-10 out of his grasp. It spun away, seemingly sucked into the darkness beyond the doorway.

The metal door stood open and flapping. Now the sound of the speeding train was enormously loud.

Dodging, Joe swung the basket again.

The phony granny glasses flew free, hitting the corridor floor. As the two struggled, the glass lenses were stomped into crunchy fragments.

Joe fought desperately. At least he had succeeded in moving the fight away from the doorway. His opponent fell backward, cracking his head on the wall. Joe moved forward, confident of victory. Unfortunately, he walked right into his enemy's last attack.

An outflung foot caught Joe in the waist. The blow took the wind out of him and sent him staggering backward.

He tried to grab the sides of the doorway. Instead he caught only chilly air.

Joe went sailing off the train.

He twisted as he fell, landing on his side with a tremendous jolt. Landing on a slanting, pebbly slope beyond the tracks, he went rolling downward about fifty feet. Finally he came to a stop beside a dark roadway.

The train went roaring on its way without him.

*   *   *

Frank looked out the compartment window as the train slowed to stop at a small rural station. The brightly lit platform was empty except for a fat man in a long black overcoat. He wore a checkered cap with earflaps and was holding an empty bird cage. Two passengers got off the train, both bundled in shapeless overcoats. Soon the train was pulling out of the station, and they were rolling again through the darkness.

"I guess Joe found his drink, and a place to sit down and enjoy it," Karen said, glancing at her watch.

"When it comes to finding supplies or a place to hang out, Joe has a sixth sense," Frank told her. "He probably found—" Frank managed to cut his voice off before he said, "some pretty girl." Instead, he finished the sentence with, "—a snack to go with his drink."

"You're probably right," Karen said.

Frank sighed. This had been an especially rough day—getting rapped in the head, running around, spending long hours searching for clues. The sounds of the train wheels on the tracks began slowly fading. The rattling and the swaying died down.

With another sigh Frank's head dipped forward.

Karen's hazel eyes were troubled. "He's been gone quite a while," she said quietly, not wanting to wake Frank.

Karen watched the darkness roll by outside

for a few more minutes. Finally she got to her feet. "I think I'll go looking for him."

The next thing Frank knew, he was being roughly shaken.

"Wake up! Wake up!" a frantic female voice cried in his ear.

"Who? What?" Frank said fuzzily.

"Joe's not in the dining car. I don't think he's on the train."

Frank licked his lips and blinked. His eyes finally focused, and he recognized Karen. Her words still hadn't penetrated. "What do you mean?" he asked.

"Joe is gone."

Rising to his feet, Frank rubbed the back of his neck. "I must have dozed off," he admitted. "Joe's in the dining car."

"No, he's *not*." Karen was shaking with tension. "I checked with the dining car, and Joe never made it there. Nobody's seen him. He's not in any of the compartments."

"Take it easy, Karen. I'll go take a look around." Still feeling a little drowsy, Frank got to his feet. "Maybe he just stepped into a washroom."

"He didn't. I had the conductor check them all out." She was pacing around the compartment. "We'll have to stop the train."

Now Frank headed for the door. "Wait on

that. I'll go hunt for some trace of Joe and ask a few questions."

Karen's voice was high. "They either threw Joe off the moving train or bundled him off at one of the stops. He could be—"

Frank cut her off. "Sit down. Wait for me here. Don't panic."

He left the compartment. Fifteen minutes later he returned, looking worried.

"You didn't find him, did you?"

"There's no sign of Joe on this train." Frank sat down quietly opposite the nervous girl. "Nobody saw him talking to anyone. Nobody saw anyone grabbing him, and nobody saw Joe get off the train at any of the stations."

Karen was back on her feet again. "Joe could be lying by the tracks, all broken and bloody, somewhere back there." She flung an arm at the darkness outside. "Or they've got him tied up in a car somewhere. Face it, Frank. We've got to stop the train."

"That won't do much good."

She stared at Frank in disbelief. "But he's your brother! He may be in big trouble!"

"Listen, please. If Joe was grabbed and taken off this train, it has to be Hawkins's men who did the job."

"I know! That's why we have to stop the train and hurry back!"

"Why?" Frank asked bluntly. "The odds are

they're taking him to Beswick. And that's where we're heading."

"They might just murder him and bury him in the woods."

"So far they haven't killed anybody. Smart thieves don't go around murdering people—it gets the police too annoyed with them."

Frank took a deep breath, still trying to get his brains to work. "What we have to do is get to Beswick and find Hawkins's hideout, his base of operations. Joe will be there."

"Aren't you worried about him?" Karen demanded.

Frank's head snapped around. "Of course I'm worried. But Joe knows how to take care of himself. I'm betting he can handle whatever situation he's in." He was on his feet, too, pacing the small compartment. "Halting the train and searching all the tracks and stations for thirty or forty miles back will take up time we don't have."

"I hope you're right," Karen said, folding her arms.

Frank nodded, his face grim. "I hope so, too."

Joe stayed where he was for a moment or two, taking stock of his situation. Although he was sore and battered, nothing important seemed broken or seriously hurt. He got up on his hands and knees, pushed, and stood up.

As far as he could tell, he was standing beside a narrow country road. The shadowy outlines of trees and hedges were all he could make out in the dark fields. Far off in the night glowed a few tiny lights that might be farmhouses or cottages.

His stiff muscles protested as he forced himself into movement. Looks like I have a hike ahead of me, he thought.

Joe thrust his hands into his pockets and started trudging along the road. The chilly night breeze was against him. He'd banged his left knee while rolling downhill. It twinged with every limping step he took.

Joe had no idea where he was, but he figured the road had to lead somewhere. At some point he'd encounter an outpost of civilization—a town, a village, a railroad station.

"Wish I'd gotten that drink. Cross-country walking is thirsty work," he muttered.

The road didn't seem very popular. Not a single car passed in either direction.

A half mile from where he'd taken his dive from the train, Joe saw a big black form beside the road. Then he realized it was a car—a large black car, lights out, waiting for something.

The words of his attempted kidnapper came back to Joe now. This must be the car that was supposed to meet them, Joe thought. Deciding he'd better avoid it, Joe ducked off for the woodlands that lined the road. He hadn't gone three steps before he stepped on a dead branch that broke with a loud snap.

The side door of the car flew open, and a gruff voice called out, "Did ya get us one of them, Willie?"

"Ar," answered Joe. He was almost behind the big auto, closer to the woods than the car.

"Which one is it—Frank or Joe Hardy?"

"How do I bloomin' know?" Joe snarled. He hoped he was making his voice sound pretty close to that of his almost-kidnapper.

"Well, don't stand there like a bump on a log. Bring whoever it is over here. Now."

Instead Joe darted for the woods, away from the car. Behind him he heard the car door slam. He ran on.

The next sound Joe heard was a pistol shot.

Chapter

12

IT WAS NEARLY DAWN when Frank and Karen arrived at the small ramshackle hotel two miles from the Beswick train station. The lobby was done in white plaster with moldings on the walls and looked as if it hadn't been renovated since the turn of the century.

Up from behind the ancient mahogany registration desk popped the bald head of a man of about sixty. "Ah, newlyweds, I wager," he said, rubbing his plump hands together and chuckling. "Run off and eloped, have you? Well, you couldn't have picked a more scenic spot. Ah, yes, Beswick is an idyllic little place, and the Winterbotham Wayside Hotel is, if I do say so myself, a jewel in the crown of this quaint and attractive village. I happen to be Winterbotham himself." He chuckled once more and slid the leather-bound register across the desk toward them.

"Good morning, Mr. Winterbotham," Frank said. "We'd like separate rooms."

"Don't tell me you're at odds already—and your honeymoon barely under way."

"We're not married. We're here on business."

"Business, you say? Well, then, let me assure you that Winterbotham's Wayside Hotel is known throughout the county of Kent as the businessman's haven." The plump proprietor nodded vigorously. "You'll find us ideally equipped for every kind of commercial endeavor. There are, to cite only one of a multitude of examples, telephones in nearly every room."

He glanced at Frank as if he expected an argument. "The telephone, as I needn't point out to a clever young businessman such as yourself, is a boon to the transacting of business. In addition, there is a very efficient manual typewriter on the premises, and it is available at any hour of the day or night, at a nominal fee, for the typing of the most demanding business documents."

Frank stared tiredly at the man until the speech was finished. "Fine," he said. "Do you have two rooms available?"

"I believe I can accommodate you and the young lady, sir. Yes, I can put you in executive suites twenty-two and twenty-five, which are right next door to each other, in spite of the numbers.''

As he signed the register, Frank leaned across the counter. "You seem to know the town well. Are you familiar with Emily Cornwall?"

"Ah, yes, the poor lass," Winterbotham said, sighing. "Miss Emily arrived a matter of two weeks ago and took up residence in the Talbot mansion."

Karen came over, yawning, and signed her name. "Would you mind if I went up to my room, Frank? Otherwise I'm going to zonk out right here."

"Could we have Ms. Kirk's key? Then you could go on with this interesting story."

"Of course. Nearly asleep on her feet, she is." Winterbotham reached into a cubbyhole behind him. "Here you are, miss, room twenty-five. Do you wish me to see you up?"

"No, I'll find my own way," Karen said, taking the heavy brass key.

"Here are the stairs. Climb but two flights and go left from the landing."

"Got it." Karen glanced back, her eyes heavy. "I'll see you in the morning sometime, Frank."

"A very charming young lady," commented Winterbotham after Karen had departed. "Now, where was I?"

"The Talbot mansion," Frank said.

"It's a huge old pile set in the middle of a

dozen bleak acres beyond the moors outside of town. Miss Emily has had few visitors and is said to be ailing. Very rich she is, but then money can't buy good health, as many another has learned. Nor good luck either, considering the accident just the other day.''

"What sort of accident?" Frank wanted to know.

"Oh, now, it wasn't the young lady, it was her companion, Miss Sheridan." Winterbotham nodded vigorously. "Poor woman was struck down near the shops by a hit-and-run driver while she was out marketing. She languishes at the moment in a hospital two villages away."

"Who's looking after Emily Cornwall?"

"Ah, she had a bit of luck there—was able to hire someone locally to see to her needs until the injured lady is up and about again." He frowned, trying to remember. "A young woman, I believe, named Miss Forman."

"How lucky," Frank said. "Any other new arrivals in town?"

"Well, there's that Professor Hobart," the hotel proprietor answered. "He arrived a month or so ago, just before poor Miss Emily. Leased the old Oscard estate. That's the place most folk hereabouts call Castle Fear."

"Spooky name. Why do they call it that?"

"It's a grim, gray, bleak place, hundreds of years old, perched on a cliff overlooking the sea." Winterbotham shook his head. "Some say

THE HARDY BOYS CASEFILES

it's haunted. There are also those who say it was a smuggler's den in days gone by. Myself, I believe both stories and don't go near there after dark." He smiled a little shamefacedly. "Nor by day, I have to admit. Too many secret passages, tunnels, and such-like around Castle Fear. I wouldn't want to fall into one, not I."

"What's Professor Hobart supposed to be up to?"

"Writing a book, he says, about local folk customs. If you ask me, the folk around here don't have a single custom worth reading about, unless you're daft." Winterbotham shook his head. "And for the life of me I can't see why the professor needs half a dozen burly lads hanging about if all he does is scribble. But I'm the first to admit I've never tried to write a book. Perhaps he's got them keeping the roof up. The whole castle is in a shocking state. I'm surprised it hasn't tumbled down before now."

"Have you seen the professor?"

"Just the once," Winterbotham said. "He's not a bad-looking chap—tall, thin, and blond, with a bit of a mustache. Talked with him a bit about local customs. But I had the impression that he and I would never be close friends, if you know what I mean."

Frank stepped back from the registration desk. "How would I get to Castle Fear?"

Winterbotham stared at him. "You're not

thinking of going there, lad. Not after what I've just told you."

"Actually, you made it sound quite interesting," Frank assured him. "I'm not at all sleepy, and a stroll is just what I need before turning in."

Sighing, Winterbotham ducked below the desk. He reappeared with a large flashlight and a knobby walking stick. "Better take these with you, sir, if you're going near Castle Fear."

Daylight came slowly, fighting its way through the heavy sea mist that hung over the countryside. Frank, swinging the borrowed walking stick, was working his way down the winding wooded path that led to the cliffside where Castle Fear stood. Though he couldn't see the ocean through the chilly fog, the salty scent of it was heavy in the air. From the distance came the cries of sea gulls.

Frank recalled the hotel proprietor's description of Professor Hobart, which came awfully close to describing the picture he'd seen of Nigel Hawkins. And the old castle sounded like a perfect headquarters for an illegal operation. Especially with lots of smugglers' tunnels for easy getaways.

Frank was moving briskly along the path. He was worried about Joe. He was sure his brother wasn't dead. Hawkins and his crew could have seen to that easily enough at several points along the line. For instance, they could have captured Joe, Karen, and himself right on the train. Instead, only one of them had been grabbed. That meant Hawkins wanted someone to question, to see how much they knew.

They'd be rough on Joe, to make him talk. So Frank had to get him out of Castle Fear as soon as he could. When he'd stepped out of the hotel, Frank had thought for a moment of going to the local police. But he could imagine the look on the local constable's face when he showed him a couple of pictures of Emily Cornwall and accused this Professor Hobart of kidnapping his brother.

Police were usually a bit short on patience and understanding—especially when you came to them with a farfetched story and no proof. Besides, Professor Hobart, although a recent arrival, was a local resident, while Frank was nothing but an outsider.

No, Frank had decided to gamble on a quick raid, figuring a single intruder had a better chance of getting into the castle without arousing guards.

Frank was clear of the woods now, making his way down a steep, grassy hillside. His target began to loom out of the fog, at first just as darker gray patches in the milky gray of the sea mist.

The place was huge, made up of dark gray blocks of stone dappled with greenish moss—it would make for slippery climbing. Towers rose up at the corners of the outer walls, and up from the main keep inside. Frank could make out narrow windows with rusted iron grilles set in them. They offered no way in. As he scanned the once-impregnable walls, however, he spotted several sections that had fallen away into ruin. High up in the castle's keep, he saw a few lights showing in windows.

Carefully Frank took a zigzagging course down the fog-ridden hillside.

The screeches of the sea gulls were louder, and he could hear the surf pounding at the rocky beach hundreds of feet below the cliff edge.

Frank reached the wall and worked along beside it. He'd noticed a dark gap that wasn't near any of the overlooking lit windows. Yes, he could climb up on the crumbling stone here and get inside.

And nobody would even know he was there.

Frank was already scaling the pile of rubble when a dark figure came flying out of the gap.

Before Frank could raise a hand to defend himself, a shoulder smashed into him.

Together with his phantom attacker Frank tumbled to the ground.

Chapter

13

JOE HARDY STOOD with his back pressed to a tree trunk. His chest burned from his run into the forest. But he didn't gulp air greedily. Instead he kept his breathing shallow, straining his ears for the sound of the guy chasing him.

He'd been zigzagging through the dark woods for nearly ten minutes. By now he figured he must have gotten a good distance between himself and that creep with the gun.

He grinned as he heard the pursuer go crashing past a hundred yards to his left. The man was muttering to himself, cursing, plunging on deeper into the dark woods.

Joe said to himself, "This would be a good time to double back."

After listening for another few seconds, he nodded and started back the way he'd come.

Behind him, the man with the pistol plowed his way deeper into the trees. He obviously had no idea where Joe was.

Joe reached the road. The car still stood on the grassy edge. Its front passenger door still hung open, spilling the faint glow of the dome light into the night.

Crouched low, Joe approached the car as if he were stalking a very dangerous animal. It would be embarrassing to lose one gunman, only to be nailed by another one still sitting in the car.

But when he finally peeked inside, the car turned out to be empty.

He eased up to the driver's side and peered in. Then he quietly opened the door, slid behind the wheel, and laughed.

"You should never leave your keys in the ignition," he said aloud as he reached across to catch the handle of the opposite door and shut it. "I mean, that gives people ideas about stealing your car."

The engine was very quiet. Joe was hardly aware that it had started. He strapped on the seat belt, gave a lazy salute in the direction of his stumbling pursuer, and drove off down the road.

Joe got lost twice on the winding country roads and wound up seeing a lot more of the nighttime Kentish scenery than he wanted to. At dawn he found himself in a village—but it wasn't Beswick.

A helpful constable who was walking his bicycle along a tree-lined lane gave Joe detailed directions on how to find his way. The police officer wasn't at all interested in Joe's borrowed auto.

The instructions worked out perfectly, and at a few minutes past eight in the morning, Joe rolled into Beswick. The day was gray and overcast. The village, which resembled the last two Joe had wandered through, had a gloomy feel to it.

Parking the car near the railroad station, Joe set off on foot down toward the center of town. The village was coming to life. Shopkeepers were removing shutters, putting out their wares, sweeping the sidewalk. Joe was still limping from his jump off the train. He was glad when the first inn came into view—the Winterbotham Wayside Hotel.

Joe was heading for the front door, eager for a chance to sit down and get some breakfast. Before he got to it, the door snapped open, and Karen Kirk came tearing out.

She bumped smack into Joe, stared in disbelief, and jumped back. "Joe! You're alive!"

Looking himself up and down, Joe said, "As far as I know."

"But what happened to you?"

"Well, I sort of left the train—um, unexpectedly," he answered. "I'll fill you and Frank in over breakfast."

"That's just it." Karen's face was pale as she grabbed Joe's arm. "Frank is gone."

"Gone where?" He guided Karen over to a wooden bench by the doorway and sat her down.

"We got to town three or four hours ago. I went up to get some sleep. That's what I thought Frank would be doing, too, as soon as the man who runs the hotel—Mr. Winterbotham—stopped talking his ear off."

"But Frank didn't go to bed."

Karen nodded. "According to Winterbotham, he borrowed a flashlight and a walking stick and headed for a place called Castle Fear."

"Doesn't sound like a tourist joint," Joe said.

Karen filled him in on the other information the proprietor had given her. "This Professor Hobart sounds like he must be Nigel Hawkins."

"So Frank, figuring that Jillian and Jed were being held at the castle, went there to take a look around," Joe finished.

"He thought you were there, too," Karen added. "I mean, we figured you'd been kidnapped off the train and taken to Hawkins's headquarters. As soon as Frank learned about Castle Fear, he must have gone right over there."

Joe shook his head. "And this is the guy who told *me* to cool it when I ran after the clown who shot at us."

"Frank left hours ago, and he hasn't come back." Karen looked worried. "We've got to get to the castle right away."

"We're not even sure anything's happened to him. Frank may just be looking around—and we might call attention to him."

"What is it with you guys? Don't you ever worry about each other? I'd say three hours was a long time to just be looking around."

"Sure, it's possible something happened to Frank and he's a prisoner now, too." Joe shook his head. "If we're going to storm a castle with just the two of us, we're going to have to make preparations."

"We'll give Frank a few more hours. In the meantime, we'll visit the local library—maybe the church as well." He got to his feet. "We also have some social calls to make. I passed an interesting-looking little restaurant on the way here. They were just opening up. Let's go get some breakfast."

"How can you eat at a time like this?"

"Hey, it's breakfast time. That's a great time for eating breakfast," Joe said. "Besides, assaulting a joint with a name like Castle Fear isn't a job I'd like to do on an empty stomach."

Frank Hardy found himself in a scrambling struggle outside the ruined gray battlements of Castle Fear. He'd taken one punch and given the dark figure in front of him two before he realized who he was fighting. "Jed—Jed! It's me, Frank Hardy."

The actor stepped back, stopping in midair the punch he'd been aiming at Frank's face. "Sorry. I thought you were one of the goons here." Jed looked around. "Have you brought the cops with you?"

"I'm by myself. I just heard about Castle Fear and—"

"That's what they call this dump?"

"It's the name the local folks around here gave it." Frank's mind was on other things. "What did you see inside? Was my brother in there? Have you seen Jillian?"

"Your brother?"

Shannon looked confused, and Frank couldn't really blame him. "They grabbed Joe a little while after they got you."

Jed shook his head. "I didn't see Joe—or Jillian, either. Some of those clowns were talking about her, though. She's in the castle someplace—they've got her locked up."

He talked in nervous jerks, his face tight. "It's all about some kind of scam they've got going on, and they're going to use Jillian in some way. I don't like this at all, Frank. They're talking about *making* her do whatever they've got in mind."

Frank cut off the excited actor. "How did you manage to get away?"

Jed pointed back at the castle. "The bars on my window were loose," he explained. "A few hours of working on them, and I was able to squeeze out. As for the rest"—he shrugged with a slightly embarrassed smile—"the stuff about me doing my own stunts—well, it's not just publicity garbage. I really do them. The jump into the courtyard wasn't so hard—I've done worse for the cameras. After that it was just a case of running for the nearest break in the wall."

"How did they manage to get you in London?" Frank asked.

"That was really stupid." Jed's ears were turning pink. "I was lured into this—um—business office, and these two guys jumped me on the stairway."

"We know about Bert Dickens—your other private eye."

Shannon's ears went pinker. "Hey, look, I wanted as many people out looking for Jillian as possible. Dickens was highly recommended by a publicity guy in London."

Jed quickly changed the subject. "Anyway, the goons knocked me out, and I woke up here. How did you find me?"

"We can talk about that later." Frank was already picking up his flashlight and walking stick, which had been knocked to the ground by Jed's initial attack. "Right now we have to get back to the village and alert—"

"I think you two would be much wiser to head back into the castle," a cultured British voice boomed out from behind them. "And be quick about it."

The voice took on a steely edge. "I'd rather hate to be forced to shoot you out in the open."

Chapter

14

JOE LEANED BACK in his chair, disappointment showing on his face. "Looks to me like nobody in all of England knows how to make an English muffin," he said, wiping his mouth on his linen napkin.

"That sure didn't stop you from finishing off three of them." Karen Kirk was drumming her fingers on the tabletop.

"Well, that's just common courtesy," Joe explained. "It's impolite not to eat what's put down before you."

She sipped her tea, glancing at her wristwatch at the same time. "What sort of social calls did you have in mind?"

"I'd like to visit Emily Cornwall. Do you know where she's staying?"

Karen sighed. "Oh, yes. Mr. Winterbotham told me all about that—for just about forever."

She pointed down the road they were facing. "Emily Cornwall is living at the Talbot estate, out beyond the edge of the village. Her longtime companion isn't with her, though."

"How come?"

"The poor woman got bounced around by a reckless driver. She's in the hospital with a broken leg."

"I'll bet our Emily was able to get a new companion, though."

"Right," Karen said. "It's a local woman named Miss Forman."

"Who no doubt is on Hawkins's payroll."

"You think so?"

"Kind of a coincidence otherwise." Joe rested both elbows on the tabletop. "Hawkins needs to have somebody near Emily."

"If Miss Forman is working for him, that will make our business a little tricky, Joe."

He just grinned. "That's the whole challenge." His grin slipped a little. "First, though, we have to drop in on the local library."

"Okay," Karen finally said. "I know that journalists are supposed to start off with research. But why is a detective so interested in the Beswick library?"

"It's a terrible secret," Joe told her, his eyes

twinkling. "I've always had this thing for musty old books."

Frank Hardy and Jed Shannon found themselves staring down the barrel of a Luger pistol.

The man who held the gun was Nigel Hawkins. "You young chaps have caused me no end of trouble." Hawkins had only one eyebrow raised, and he held the Luger rock-steady. But the look in his eyes said that he'd easily kill them if they tried anything.

Hawkins continued in a smooth, almost chatty tone. "I mean really, dear boys, you've come uncomfortably close to throwing a wrench in the works."

Frank knew his face was pale, but he tried to sound as calm as Hawkins when he spoke. "The wrench has already been tossed, Nigel. Before I headed up here this morning, I stopped at the Beswick police station."

"Did you now?"

"If I don't get in touch with them within an hour, they'll be out here in force."

Hawkins had a harsh, nasal laugh. "Nice try, m'lad," he said. "Unfortunately for you, though, I overheard you telling good old Jed here that you hadn't talked to the local coppers. So if you'll be so kind as to climb through this break in the wall . . ."

"Okay, maybe I was bluffing about the

police," Frank said. "But I'm here with some-one who'll go to the police if I don't turn up."

"You mean Karen Kirk? Oh, yes," Hawkins said, smiling at the look on Frank's face. "I know all about the young lady. And I sincerely hope she doesn't try what you're suggesting."

Hawkins smiled like a cat waiting outside a mouse hole. "You see, I have someone watch-ing over her. He knows what she looks like—but she doesn't know him." Hawkins's smile grew colder. "She won't even know what hit her."

He gestured with the gun. "Enough chat, I think. March along now, lads."

Hawkins kept them covered all the way into the ancient keep and down a dark hallway that ended in a thick walnut door. Leaning against the gray stone wall was a big, wide man in a black pullover and dark jeans. He had close-cropped graying hair and a broken nose.

"Limehouse, old man," Hawkins greeted the big man who threw the door open. The two pris-oners were confronted with a long flight of chipped stone steps leading to a lower level of the castle.

"Escort these two reckless lads the rest of the way down and lock them into one of our cozier dungeon cells."

"Can I knock them around a little?" Lime-house inquired in a rough, growling voice. He sounded a little too eager to Frank.

Hawkins poked his tongue into his cheek, staring up at the low, damp ceiling. "Not just yet, Limehouse," he said. "Keep in mind that our friend Mr. Shannon's face is his fortune. We wouldn't want to force him into a new line of work. I mean, he's doing so well as a movie star."

"I could hit him in lots of places besides his face," the big man offered. "Places where it wouldn't show."

"No, don't hit either of them for a while," Hawkins instructed his henchman. "Mind you, if they try to escape, then do as you see fit. Short of killing them, though. One hates to resort to murder."

Limehouse lifted a snub-nosed .38 revolver from the waistband of his trousers. "Okay, kiddies, start down those steps," he ordered. "Single file, and no funny stuff. You can't be much of a movie star if you don't have any kneecaps."

"So I've heard." Jed's voice was little more than a mutter as he started the trek downward.

Joe Hardy sneezed.

The two old ladies dozing over their magazines snapped awake to glare at him. They didn't have far to frown. The small library was only a single room lined with light oak bookshelves.

"Dust," Joe apologized, pointing to the scatter of old papers and charts spread across the table in front of him. He smiled as charmingly as possible and went back to taking notes.

Karen Kirk was pretending to browse, moving around the bookshelves with her hands behind her back. She eased over to one of the bow windows in the small room, taking a careful glance out into the street.

Returning to Joe's side, she whispered, "How's the old research coming?"

"I've got just about everything we need."

Sitting, she moved her chair up next to his. Her voice was even softer as she whispered in his ear, "I think somebody is following us."

"You mean the little guy in the raincoat?"

She pulled back. "You noticed him already?"

"He was watching us outside the hotel, loitering around the restaurant, then tailed us here."

Karen was looking distinctly unhappy. "What are we going to do?"

Joe grinned. "How are you at fainting?"

"Beg pardon?"

He spelled it out for her. "Can you pretend to faint?"

"I suppose so, but Jillian's the actress, not me. Should I try it right here?"

"Save your acting juices," Joe told her with a grin. "Go out the front door of the library. Look excited, like you had to get someplace important in a hurry. Turn down that alley we saw, next to the butcher shop. Once you're sure the man in the raincoat is following you, faint and fall down when you're halfway down the alley."

Karen gave him a dubious look. "You realize that alley is going to be pretty dirty."

"Just do it, okay?"

"All right, but wallowing in garbage isn't my idea of fun."

"Look, you ruined that raincoat when we hit the dirt last night," Joe said, his face suddenly grim, "and wallowing in crud is a lot more fun than getting kidnapped or shot."

Joe quietly headed out the back door of the library. Moving in a slight crouch, he slipped behind the high hedge surrounding the small front lawn. From there, unobserved, he could watch the man in the tan raincoat.

He was beginning to suspect that he'd met the person tailing them before. This was the same guy who, disguised as a little old lady, had given him a quick flying lesson off the train last night.

The front door of the library swung open, and Karen, looking excited and upset, came hurrying out. She started walking rapidly toward the local police station, her heels clicking on the sidewalk. Her eyes stared straight ahead, as if she was intent on reaching there as soon as she possibly could.

The small man in the long, flapping raincoat hesitated, frowning across at the doorway of the library. Then, when he saw where Karen was heading, he tightened the belt of his coat and took off after her. Joe noticed that he stayed on the opposite side of the street, walking at a slower pace so he could keep an eye on Karen.

Joe waited.

As soon as Karen stepped into the alley, her shadow crossed to the other sidewalk and started after her.

119

Chapter

15

THE MAN IN THE RAINCOAT had his eyes only on the girl.

Joe sprinted across the street. By the time he reached the mouth of the alley, Karen was going into her fainting act. She did it very convincingly, swaying, taking a few staggering steps, trying to steady herself against the brick wall. Then, dropping to her knees, she toppled forward.

The man who was trailing her froze in surprise. Then he ran toward the fallen girl. Joe smiled. As he expected, the guy was completely fooled.

Putting on another burst of speed, Joe came up on the man and jabbed two fingers hard in his back. "Very slowly, raise both your hands and lock them behind your head." Joe's muscles tensed as he waited for the response. If the guy didn't buy his phony gun, he'd have to throw him into a wall.

"The lass has fainted. I was only trying to lend a hand."

"I want both of them behind your head!" Joe growled. "I recognized you in the street, Granny."

The little man seemed to shrink into himself. He also raised both hands.

At the same time, Karen stood up, brushing her skirt. "I fell right on top of a melon rind," she said accusingly to Joe.

"Frisk him" was all Joe said.

Karen made a face and searched the man. She located a .32 revolver and a switchblade knife. Moving around behind their prisoner, Karen turned the weapons over to Joe.

"We're going to leave you in this alley for now."

"Don't shoot me, lad. I treated you well last night, didn't I?"

"Sure. Nobody ever gave me a nicer order to jump off a moving train before." Joe's voice was grim as he prodded the man with the gun barrel. "Take off the raincoat."

"You want my raincoat?"

"I'm going to borrow it for a while."

"How in the bloomin'—"

THE HARDY BOYS CASEFILES

"Hurry up and get out of it. We still have to tie you up and gag you."

The gunman's voice was sharp. "Leaving me lying about in this alley isn't going to sit right with certain people."

"I know," Joe told him. "That's one of the reasons I'm doing it."

At a few minutes past noon the silence of the Castle Fear dungeons was broken by footsteps. Inside the damp, gray cell Frank Hardy turned from staring at the slightly slimy stone wall in front of him. Jed Shannon was already standing by the door, where a key was rattling in the lock.

Limehouse, Nigel Hawkins's hulking thug, swung the door open with one hand. His other held a gun on them. "Let's go, boys," he ordered, gesturing with the pistol. "You're wanted upstairs."

"For what?" asked Jed.

"You're playing the wrong part, actor." The broken-nosed thug pointed to the stairway. "You got no lines to ask questions in this script."

Prodded by Limehouse, Jed and Frank climbed the stone steps. They marched along a paneled hallway on the ground floor of Castle Fear, then into a large, beam-ceilinged room. French doors let wan sunlight into the room, and even though it was summer, a fire crackled in the hearth on the far wall.

Jed stood in the doorway staring at the slender blond girl sitting at an enormous dining table. "Jillian!"

She was a very pretty young woman with shoulder-length blond hair, although just now her face was pale and there were shadows under her eyes. That gave her an even stronger resemblance to Emily Cornwall.

She stared as if she were seeing a ghost when Jed appeared. For a second the glow in Jillian's face made her look incredibly beautiful. Then it disappeared, like a light that had been abruptly shut off, as her face crumpled into tears. Jed dashed over to throw his arms around her. "Jillian!"

"Jed, I'm sorry about all this," Jillian sobbed as she nestled into his chest. "I was stupid to let Nigel fool me into coming down here."

"Jillian, I—" Jed began. Frank had never seen the young star's face look so tender—and he was convinced Jed wasn't calling on his acting ability.

"That's enough clinching for now," a brisk voice called out. Nigel Hawkins stood at the head of the table. "Please break it up and take your places."

"You're holding us prisoner, but you're serving us lunch?" Frank stared in disbelief at the elaborate place settings around the large oak table.

"Why ever not?" Hawkins seated himself. "You'll find that I'm quite a civilized fellow—when people don't annoy me. And dear Jillian can tell you that I'm extremely thoughtful. Jillian, sit at my right, if you would. Mr. Shannon is on your right, with Mr. Hardy opposite him. Limehouse, you'll keep an eye on our guests. And Rowland, you'll sit next to Mr. Hardy."

Another man came into the dining room. It was the same large, red-faced blond guy who'd pretended to be Ian Fisher-Stone, Jillian's agent. "Such a pleasure to see you again, Hardy," the man said. "How's the head?"

"Fine, now," Frank told him. "You're a regular artist with a blackjack." The man smiled, and Frank decided to try another question. "Where's the real Fisher-Stone?"

"In the south of France." Rowland sat down.

"By choice?"

"Oh, yes. He chose quite readily. All he needed was a little persuasion—and the wherewithal—and he was most delighted to leave London."

Hawkins slid his damask napkin out of its silver ring, snapped it to unfurl it, and draped it over his right knee. "Why use violence when a simple bribe will do?" he said to Frank. "Unfortunately, we were informed that you and your brother were above that sort of thing."

Rowland smiled. "That's why we resorted to scare tactics."

Frank took his seat. "Once this is all over, what do you intend to do?" he asked. "Shake hands all around and drive off into the sunset?"

Hawkins picked up a small silver bell and rang it once. "You have the foolish notion that we can't afford to leave any live witnesses behind to identify us. Is that it?"

"Seems obvious." Frank shrugged. "You've already done something to my brother."

"I most certainly have not," Hawkins told him haughtily. "Oh, we *tried* to spirit him off the train last night. But he eluded my man, apparently diving from the train on his own. I have no idea as to his present whereabouts."

"He also stole one of our cars," Rowland added. "Seems a resourceful young man."

Frank was relieved that Joe was alive and that he wasn't a prisoner someplace in the castle. That is, if Hawkins was telling the truth. "Okay, so what do you intend to do with us?" Frank asked.

"After Jillian has done her bit, you'll all be free to go," Hawkins assured him. "I take that back—actually, you'll be chained up in this frightful old castle. After we're safely out of the country, the authorities will be notified to come and claim you."

"But we can identify you, tell the police who stole the Talbot emeralds."

Hawkins laughed. "We're never returning to England, dear boy. You'd be surprised at how many countries are friendly to men of means. Warm countries where there's never a wisp of beastly fog or so much as a suggestion of a snowflake."

"You're giving up your show-business career, Hawkins?" asked Jed, who was sitting next to the young actress, holding her hand.

"You mean those wretched films I produced?" Hawkins laughed. "Let's face it, the emeralds will gross more than those movies."

An ancient servant came tottering into the dining room, carrying a large silver tureen of steaming soup. He began ladling it out into the soup plates, starting with Hawkins.

"People warned me," Jillian said to Jed, her eyes shining with tears. "But I kept on believing Mr. Hawkins was really making a big-budget film with me as the star. I studied Emily Cornwall's life, took photos wearing a black wig. I even made a sample videotape as Emily."

"She's quite a remarkable actress," Hawkins said as he tasted his soup. "If I planned to stay in the movie business, I truly believe I could make her into a major star."

"They're going to substitute me for Emily." Jillian lowered her head, not looking Jed in the eye. "I'm to go to the solicitors, pass myself off as her, and collect the jewels."

"That won't work," Jed objected. "They won't turn the emeralds over to her."

Hawkins smiled. "Keep in mind, my boy, that no one has seen little Emily for years. She's been ill, living abroad as something of a hermit."

"What about fingerprints?" Jed objected.

"None exist. At least not anywhere her solicitors can get hold of them."

Jed said triumphantly, "Handwriting."

"They've made me practice her signature." Jillian rubbed her hand. "She broke some bones in an accident. If anyone asks about the writing, I'm supposed to use that as an excuse. Jed, once I realized what they really had in mind, I told them I wanted no part of it."

"That's why they kidnapped you, Jed," Frank broke in angrily. "For a little leverage."

Near the door, Limehouse cleared his throat, swinging his gun toward Jed. "Would be a shame if anything were to happen to him."

"It would certainly ruin a lot of careful planning," Hawkins said. "Machinery I put together after seeing Jillian in some dreadful play a few weeks ago—what was it?"

" *'Tis a Pity She Won't Be Woo'd,*" Frank said.

"Awful thing. But it introduced me to Ms. Jillian Seabright. I mean there I was, suffering through that awful play that would have been better left buried in Britain's musty theatrical past. Then I realized this sweet young thing was a near double for Emily Cornwall. Of course, I knew about the emeralds, and that no one had seen Emily for many a moon.''

"We keep extensive files," Rowland explained. "Dear Emily is only one of those people whose fortunes we—ah, monitor.''

"Monitor, then steal," Frank said.

Hawkins waved a playful finger. "Robbing the rich is an old English sport, Hardy. Started by a chap named Robin Hood. It's much more fun than making second-rate cinema offerings, or— What is it, Walter?''

A lanky man came pushing into the dining room. "Might be trouble," he said gruffly.

The teasing smile vanished from Hawkins's face. "What, exactly?''

Walter said, "We've been trying to call the Forman woman. She's supposed to be sitting on the Cornwall girl, awaiting word from us.''

"And?''

"Nobody's answering the phone there." A look of unease passed over the crook's face. "I don't like it. Something's gone wrong with the plan.''

Chapter

16

JOE PASSED the binoculars to Karen. "That's her on the terrace, all right."

Karen put the brand-new field glasses to her eyes. "Yes, she's in the wheelchair, all bundled up in plaid blankets."

"So I'd guess the lady standing next to her must be Miss Forman." Joe and Karen were stretched out in a clump of brush about a quarter of a mile from the rear of the huge, dreary, dark stone Talbot mansion. Swampy fields stretched out all around them, dotted with the occasional leafless tree. Big black crows circled low around the sprawling house, cawing and searching for a meal. "That lump in the fake companion's sweater looks like a gun."

"Can you be sure at this distance?"

"It's part keen eyesight," Joe admitted, "and part good guessing."

"Miss Forman doesn't look much like a companion—more like a barmaid who throws unruly drunks out by herself."

"We've been ducked down here since she wheeled Emily onto the terrace." Joe reclaimed the binoculars they'd bought in town after they'd stowed the gagged gunman at the end of the alley. "I don't see signs that anyone else is at home."

"So we're going through with this?"

"Keep these in your shoulder bag." Joe handed Karen the glasses, took a gray cap out of the pocket of his borrowed raincoat, and pulled it low over his eyes. "I'm taller than the guy who tailed us, but I should be able to pass for him until we're fairly close. Let's roll."

"I'm doing a lot more performing than reporting lately."

"Call it participatory journalism," Joe replied.

Karen stood up, put her hands behind her back, and began walking across the bleak fields toward the mansion.

Joe followed close behind, his head hanging low and the gun he'd taken showing plainly in his right hand. "Act frightened," he whispered.

"I don't have to act. I *am* frightened."

The crows, who had found something to eat in the tall grass, flapped away from them into the sky, cawing raucously.

Miss Forman looked up when Joe and Karen

were about five hundred feet from the wide flag-stone terrace. "Willie, you fool," she called out, hand slipping into her sweater pocket. "You weren't supposed to bring her here."

"It's working," Joe said in a tight whisper.

"You were just supposed to follow the girl and keep her away from the police." Annoyance tinged the heavyset blond woman's voice.

"Couldn't be helped," Joe muttered, his head still down.

Emily Cornwall, her mouth slightly open, stared as the two of them approached.

When Joe and Karen were about fifteen feet from the woman, she suddenly glared at them. "You're not Willie!" she exclaimed.

Karen's hands came up from behind her, flinging two fistfuls of swamp muck at Miss Forman's face. She dived at the woman, tackling her around the legs.

Joe sprinted forward, grabbing the woman's wrist before she could yank her gun free. "I wouldn't try anything foolish," he warned.

"You're one of those idiot Hardys." Miss Forman frowned but stopped trying to get her gun out.

"I am a Hardy," Joe admitted. "But I don't think you're in a position to comment on my intelligence. You can get up now, Karen."

As Karen got to her feet Joe told Miss Forman, "Slip your hand out of that pocket. And it had better come out slow and empty."

The woman glared at him but did as he said.

Reaching into the sweater pocket, Joe came out with a .22 automatic. He took a quick look in Emily's direction. "Any more of them around, Miss Cornwall?"

"Just her. Do you have any idea what's going on?" The dark-haired young woman looked very frail. The shadows under her eyes were even deeper than in the pictures Joe had seen, and her face was pale with fear.

"We'll fill you in shortly," he promised. Turning to Karen, he said, "Hold this and keep it pointed at our phony friend here." Joe handed her the .22 automatic and moved to the wheelchair. Then he asked Emily, "Are you all right?"

"Not especially, no," Emily replied. "For one thing, she's got me tied to this wheelchair. I haven't really needed it in months, but Miss Sheridan, my real companion, insisted that we bring it along."

Joe yanked away the plaid blankets and saw that the slender girl was tied hand and foot with lengths of nylon clothesline. "I'll get you out in a second," he said, taking out his pocket knife. "I'm Joe Hardy, by the way. My friend is Karen Kirk."

"I've heard about you and your brother," Emily Cornwall said. "I imagine that all this has something to do with the emeralds."

"Got it on the first guess," Joe said, sawing

at the strands of nylon. "Karen is going to stay with you, and once we get Miss Forman safely locked away, she'll fill you in on what's been going on these past few days."

Karen frowned. "You mean I'm staying here?"

"Yes, while I go over to Castle Fear."

In the sun room off the terrace the phone began to trill.

Karen glanced toward the open French doors.

"Let it ring," Joe said. "And we're changing plans—we're getting out of here right away."

Frank Hardy sat at the dining table at Castle Fear, staring at Stanley, another thug. But Frank's eyes flashed to the head of the table, where Nigel Hawkins abruptly stood up and tossed his napkin down beside his soup plate.

"You're sure you dialed it right? These blasted provincial phone exchanges." He stalked over to the doorway. "I'll try it myself. That fool woman knows her job. She's supposed to remain at the house around the clock."

After Hawkins left the room Jed turned to Rowland. "Why don't you guys just quit right now? I don't think your boss realizes that he's taken a tiger by the tail here."

"Oh, Nigel's not my boss, dear boy. We're equal partners in this venture."

"Whatever." The young actor waved his hand

impatiently. "The point is, none of you clowns seems to realize what you've done here."

Jed glanced over at his lady friend. "It's bad enough that you kidnapped Jillian, but—hey, when you snatch one of the most popular actors in the world today, you're in big trouble. My studio isn't going to let you retire to some tropical island to enjoy the warm, quiet life."

"My, such an enormous ego for one so young in years." Rowland began laughing. "Really, son, you're in no position to make threats. Not while you're a helpless prisoner in a castle that boasts a fully equipped torture chamber down in the dungeon. Did they show you that on the guided tour?"

Jed and Frank were silent.

"Nigel is something of a softy when it comes to physical violence." Rowland casually bent his heavy silver soup spoon into a U. "but as frank here can testify, I can be quite nasty if I want."

"All too true," Frank agreed. "Don't antagonize him, Jed."

"Hey, I'm not trying to rattle this guy's cage. I'm just pointing out that I don't happen to be your everyday kidnap victim. I'm a celebrity, you know. Maybe they're biting off more than they can chew."

"Jed, dear, they have a lot of very nasty people in their crew." Jillian took Jed's hand, looking frightened. "You're not going to talk them out of going ahead with this scam."

"Wisely put, little Jillian," Rowland said. "You seem much wiser than your young man. I don't understand how you manage to put up with him."

"Limehouse, Walter." The look on Hawkins's face as he hurried back in cut off further conversation. "Put all three of our guests in a cell down below. And hurry."

Rowland pushed back from the table. "Problems, Nigel?"

"I can't get an answer from that Forman woman. The phone rings and rings, but she doesn't pick up." Nigel Hawkins scowled. "Our whole plan depends on keeping Emily Cornwall quietly out of circulation on that estate, so we'll have to go over there and see if anything is amiss." He stopped next to Frank's chair. "Did your brother have something to do with this?"

Frank shrugged. "Until a little while ago I thought you had him here in the castle," he replied. "If Joe's not here, he could be roaming around doing just about anything."

"He'd better not be interfering in my plans." Hawkins's voice sounded a lot less cultured and a lot more grating. "That wouldn't be the least bit smart."

"Too bad we talked instead of eating that soup." Jed Shannon's stomach growled as he paced around the small stone room. "No telling how long we'll be stuck down here."

135

Frank was exploring the damp new cell where the three of them had been locked in. "I wonder what actually happened over at the Talbot mansion," he said, rapping at stones here and there. "More importantly, did Joe have anything to do with it?"

"The worst part is the way I've entangled the two of you in my mess." Jillian sat huddled on a stone shelf that came out of the wall. "I've never thought of myself as being self-centered, although I guess all actresses are to some degree. The more I think about this disaster, the more I realize it was vanity that got me in trouble. Because I believed I was ready to star in a movie . . ."

"Hey, you're more than ready." Jed halted beside Jillian. "I've acted with girls who weren't half as talented as you—or as beautiful."

Jillian looked down. "Thanks. But somehow, starring in a big film doesn't seem all that important right now."

"We'll get out of this," Jed promised. He glanced at Frank. "Do you believe Hawkins won't hurt us?"

"Hawkins seems to draw the line at murder."

"But that other guy—Rowland? You know, we never found out if that was his first or last name. He looks like the kind of guy who's capable of putting a bullet into any one of us." Jed began pacing again.

"I'd say he was the nastier of the two," Frank

agreed. He tapped on another of the large gray stones.

"What are you doing that for?" Jillian asked.

"This castle is supposed to have hidden rooms and secret passages," Frank replied. "I'm just checking to see if there's a forgotten exit in here."

"Why not just use the door?" a voice behind them asked.

They whirled to find Joe Hardy grinning at them from the open door of their cell.

Chapter

17

FRANK HARDY FIGURED his jaw must be hanging somewhere around his belt buckle. "J-Joe?" he finally managed. "How did *you* get here? Not that we aren't glad to see you," he quickly added. Shaking his head, Frank began to grin.

Joe pushed the heavy oak cell door all the way open, being careful not to make any noise. "Folks usually think you're the scholarly side of this team," he said, returning Frank's grin. "But I can do a little research now and then."

"Meaning?"

"I ran into Karen when I finally reached Beswick this morning—I'll tell you what happened after I—ah, left the train—later." Joe grinned. "She told me about Castle Fear, how you'd gone to scout it out and hadn't come back. I got to thinking about old castles, and that sent me to the local library. Sure enough, they had a couple of musty old books all about Castle Fear, written by a local historian about two hundred years ago. The guy must have had a lot of time on his hands—he'd drawn a complete set of architectural plans, very detailed.''

Frank had to grin. ''Detailed enough to include the locations of the secret passages and entrances?''

Joe nodded. ''Exactly. I picked an entrance that lies just on the other side of the stone wall. All I had to do was wait until nobody was around. I figured the bad guys had tossed you into a dungeon—after all, what's a castle for? After a little poking around, I found you guys.''

He turned toward the blond actress. ''I'm Joe Hardy, and you must be Jillian Seabright. You really do look a lot like Emily Cornwall.''

Jed Shannon looked impressed. ''So you've actually seen Emily Cornwall?''

''Karen and I just rescued her from a phony companion by the name of Miss Forman.''

''Where are Karen and the Cornwall girl?'' Frank wanted to know. ''You didn't leave them at the Talbot place, did you?''

''That was what I'd planned at first,'' Joe admitted. ''But then the phone started ringing, and it occurred to me that Hawkins might be checking up. If nobody answered, he'd probably send a carload of goons over to investigate.''

139

"Hawkins did *exactly* that—right after his phone call wasn't answered," Frank said.

"Well, they won't find anyone at home," Joe said. "We changed plans and loaded Miss Forman into the car I'm using at the moment." He held up a hand to cut off the questions he expected. "I'll tell you how I got hold of the car later. Anyway, Karen and Emily dropped me off within sight of Castle Fear, then took off to deliver Miss Forman to the local law."

"Then all we have to do now," said Frank, "is get ourselves out of here."

"We can get out the same way I came in." Joe tugged a small flashlight out of his pants pocket. "This way to the exit."

Single file, they left the dungeon cell with Joe in the lead, then Jillian and Jed, and Frank bringing up the rear.

As they were passing the stone stairway that led up to the ground floor, the door at its top creaked open. Framed in the light was Limehouse, staring down at them.

"Hoy!" he shouted, fumbling for his gun as he charged down the stairs. The big thug was aiming at them when Joe scooped up a rock and threw it at him like his best fastball.

Limehouse flinched back and lost his balance. The pistol flew from his hand to land with a clatter in a dark corner of the dungeon.

"Nice move, Joe," Jed Shannon said.

But Limehouse didn't fall. Moving much

faster than a man his size usually did, he thrust a hand out to grab hold of something on the wall. It broke his fall but then tore loose from the rings that had held it to the wall.

Frank sucked in his breath through his teeth when he saw what it was. Though rusty and covered with spiderwebs, the ancient battle-ax still looked lethal enough to take care of all of them.

Waving the ax above his head, Limehouse charged again.

Joe grabbed Jed's arm. "You and Jillian—down that hallway!" Then he joined Frank to meet Limehouse's rush.

Snarling in rage, Limehouse was swinging the ax like a baseball bat. The sharp edges sliced the air as he whipped the handle back and forth.

Frank and Joe had no choice—they had to retreat before the whistling blade got any closer. Unless Limehouse got tired, they wouldn't have a chance. And Limehouse didn't look as if he would tire soon.

"Plan B," Frank abruptly said.

Joe glanced at his brother. "I didn't know we had a plan— Yow!"

Limehouse was leaping for him, the ax held high. But Frank was leaping, too, coming in low under the ax. He swung his leg in a roundhouse kick, catching Limehouse behind the knees.

The big man toppled, the ax clanging against the stone wall.

Joe yanked his brother up. "This way—fast!"

They nearly crashed into Jed and Jillian, who were running the other way. "No good," Jed panted. "It's just a dead end."

"That's what you think." Joe dashed down to a seemingly solid wall, hit one of the stones, and heaved. With a grating shriek the whole wall moved, revealing a secret doorway.

Joe stepped aside, shining his flashlight into the dark hole beyond. "Watch it—there are steps right through here."

The others piled through the doorway, then Joe followed. They could hear heavy footsteps coming closer—Limehouse was back on his feet.

Joe put his shoulder to the secret door. "We've got to get this shut, and fast."

Frank added his shoulder as well.

Limehouse appeared in the corridor, still waving his ax.

"Push!" Joe urged.

Jed joined them, and the heavy door began to close. They got it shut, and a hidden lock engaged with a solid *clunk*.

They were just in time—Limehouse had arrived at the door, bashing at it furiously.

The sound was dull and muffled through the door, and soon it faded as Jed, Jillian, Frank, and Joe made their way through the dark tunnel. The smell of damp earth was strong. Somewhere unseen water was dripping on rock.

Joe was again leading the procession, lighting

the passageway ahead. "This part of the tunnel is only about a mile long, according to the map." He shone his compact flashlight around. "But it seems a lot longer in the dark."

"Sure does," Jed agreed. "We— Ouch!" He tripped over something on the rocky floor, stumbling against one of the timbers that shored up the tunnel roof. On hands and knees, he looked back at whatever had tripped him. "Shine the light over this way, Joe," he requested. "I—I'm hoping this is just a prop."

Helping the actor to his feet, Joe swept his beam around the floor. "Nope, that looks like a real human skull," he said.

"Brrrrr." Jed stared at the ancient yellow bone. "Think he was trying to get in or out?"

"It doesn't matter now," Frank said. "We'd better keep moving."

Joe moved again to the head of the parade. "Do you know that guy with the lopsided nose?"

"Hawkins calls him Limehouse."

"He must be the same one who took those shots at us at the beginning of this business."

Jillian was walking with Jed. "Did you hurt yourself?"

Jed shook his head. "Nope. Just fouled up my favorite pair of pants."

After a moment Joe announced, "Okay, folks. Looks like we've reached the end of the line."

The beam from his flashlight danced on a

rounded section of stone wall. To Frank it looked like the inside of a well.

"Where will this thing let us out?" he asked as his brother aimed the flashlight at a wooden trapdoor over their heads.

"Outside the castle wall, up near a stretch of woods." Joe grinned. "When they were really using this thing, I guess the woods were bigger and hid it better."

Frank reached up. The ceiling was low enough that he could get a grip on the metal latch handle that locked the trapdoor. "If this is out in the open, it may not be a secret anymore. Limehouse may have it staked out."

He tried to turn the handle.

"C'mon, Frank, we don't have all day," Joe urged.

Frank grunted. "Seems to be stuck."

"Here, I'll give you a hand." Joe caught hold of the ancient, rusty handle, gritting his teeth and straining.

The handle resisted for a moment, seemed to give, and then, with a metallic *twang*, broke off.

Both Hardys tumbled to the ground, the useless handle clanging on the rocky floor.

Jed had already taken their place, shoving frantically at the door. "Still jammed," he announced.

Jillian, in the rear of the group, suddenly

gasped. "I hear something," she said, "down at the other end of the tunnel. Footsteps—coming this way."

Joe picked up the now-useless door latch. "Great," he said. "Up the creek—without a handle."

Chapter

18

BOTH HARDYS JUMPED to their feet to attack the jammed trap door.

Joe pulled out his pocket knife and wedged it into the crack between the door and its frame. He strained against the latch, trying to lever the trapped tongue free.

No good. He began whacking at the knife with the broken latch handle. There was still resistance, but he thought the knife was beginning to move.

Frank grabbed a handy rock and rapped sharply at the door. Maybe the vibration would dislodge any rust stuck in the latch itself.

After a desperate couple of seconds, Joe suddenly yelled, "It's giving!" One more shot with his trusty handle and the latch gave. Jed and

Frank shoved, and with a considerable creak, the door opened upward. A large rectangle of blue afternoon sky showed in the low ceiling of the tunnel.

"Give me a leg up," Joe said.

Frank boosted his brother while Joe scrambled desperately for a hold in the grass above.

He hauled himself through the trapdoor. Then, kneeling on the edge, Joe leaned back in. "Get Jillian up here next."

Jed lifted the girl up by her waist, and she perched on Frank's shoulders to boost herself out of the opening.

Heavy footsteps echoed behind them in the darkness of the underground passageway.

Frank boosted Jed up next, and then Joe and the actor pulled Frank out.

"We'd better head for the woods," Joe said, pointing. "There's a road just beyond there where we could—"

"Trouble," Frank cut in, his eyes on the castle behind them.

Through one of the gaps in the tumbledown gray stone wall they could see Hawkins and two more of his goons. Rowland had climbed one of the solid sections of the battlement and was pointing down, directing his pals toward the escapees.

"Well, Limehouse raised the alarm—and now we're spotted," Frank said.

"I picked up a couple of guns on the way in."

Joe looked around uneasily. There was no cover nearby, nowhere they could make a stand. "I don't think they'll help us stand off a whole gang in the open."

Hawkins and his six men now had their weapons out and were climbing the rubble mounds on the other side of the castle walls.

"So," Frank said, "we've got a choice of being shot or surrendering."

Nigel Hawkins was the first to burst through the opening in the wall. "Where is she?" he demanded when he saw Joe. "What have you done with Emily Cornwall?"

A wild cry from Jillian rang out over whatever else Hawkins was going to say. "Jed, look!" she cried, grabbing his arm and pointing toward the woods beyond them.

"Hey, it's just like the movies," the actor said, laughing. "The cops arrive in the nick of time."

Coming down into the field were three uniformed police officers, and three more in plain clothes.

Face pale, Hawkins stared at the oncoming police. His carefully constructed suave mask was shattered by sheer rage. "You young fool, you've wrecked it all." He raised his gun, taking careful aim at Joe.

Frank flung the old iron handle still in his hand straight at Hawkins's gun. At the same time Joe crouched low and charged at Hawkins.

The gun went off, with one shot that went high. Joe launched himself at Hawkins, catching him in a flying tackle.

Hawkins tumbled backward into the wall of the castle. His second shot went straight up into the air.

Joe chopped at Hawkins's wrist, knocking the gun out of his hand. Frank caught the gun as Jed came up from behind Joe and delivered a punch to Hawkins's jaw.

The head crook bounced back to the wall and sank down in an unconscious sprawl.

His gang, realizing that the police were coming in for the kill, was scattering across the courtyard, heading for the cars.

Jed, with a satisfied grin, rubbed his knuckles. "See, Hardy? I really do all my own stunts."

Jillian, laughing, came up and hugged him.

Joe slumped against the wall and looked over at his brother. "Here come the police," he said. "Do you want to explain things, or should I?"

Hours later Frank and Joe were back in their London hotel. The Kent police had taken over the case in a quick and businesslike way. They'd gotten confessions from Nigel and his men regarding the letters and the phone bugs, as well as the shooting and the bomb. They admitted to kidnapping Jillian after she'd learned the role she was to play in the heist, and they had made sure there were no photos of her anywhere so no one could make a connection between her and Emily. The police had questioned Frank, Joe, Jillian, and Jed and taken their statements, and had even given their witnesses a lift to London before evening.

Joe came out of the shower humming a cheerful tune as he wandered around the room in his bathrobe. His older brother was on the telephone.

"That's great," Frank was saying. "Glad to hear it."

Moving to the window, Joe looked down into the twilit street. "Not a trace of fog," he observed happily. "It's going to be a perfect night—just exactly right for my dinner date with Karen."

After hanging up, Frank walked over to stand beside Joe. "That was Jed Shannon," he said.

"I guess Larry Berman has been busy. Jed's sure getting a lot of publicity out of this." Joe started to get dressed. "The newsstands in the streets were full of it by the time we reached town. " 'Film Star Rescues Kidnapped Actress!' " He grinned. "Not exactly true, but it makes for interesting reading."

"The stories seem to have done Jillian a lot of good, too," Frank said. "Her new agent— she'll never see that Fisher-Stone guy again— just phoned. She's gotten some great offers. Jed says his studio has just signed her up to star with him in his next picture."

"Here in England?"

"Nope, in California someplace. Jed said they'll be leaving for there after the case is all settled."

"They find each other, she gets famous, they work happily ever after. Sounds like a great ending for them." Joe pulled on his socks. "Nigel Hawkins and his gang are all in the lockup, so they can't bother Jed or Jillian anymore."

"True." Frank sat on the edge of the bed. "I hear that Emily Cornwall collected the Talbot emeralds right on schedule. She's planning to come out into the world a bit more."

"I had a hunch she would, after talking to her the other day. It looks like everything's—"

The phone rang.

Frank answered. "Hello? Oh, hi. Just a second. For you, Joe."

"Yes?" Joe said into the receiver.

"I'm really very unhappy about this." Karen Kirk's voice crackled over the phone line. "But I've got this incredible opportunity, and I just can't pass it up. My friends on one of the magazines want me to do an article on the whole Jillian Seabright case."

She sounded a little embarrassed. "You know, an 'I was there' kind of thing. Corny, maybe, but it will be a big credit for me. The problem is that I have to meet with them tonight. I just can't keep our dinner date, Joe."

"How about a late dinner instead?"

Karen sounded doubtful. "This may drag on for hours."

"Lunch tomorrow? You can interview me for your story." That sounded desperate, even to Joe.

"Tomorrow I'll already be working away on the article. There's a very tight deadline," she explained. "But I'm sure we'll be able to get together at least once before you guys leave England."

"I'm sure we will. Good luck, Karen." Joe hung up.

"No date?" asked his brother.

"I'll give you the details," Joe told him sourly. "But you've got to promise not to laugh."

Frank and Joe's next case:

The Hardys pay a visit to Bayport's newest martial arts school and find that someone's trying to run the place out of the neighborhood. The Scorpions, a tough street gang, say the building is on their turf, and the school's students have already felt the Scorpions' sting.

The home boys may want to rumble with the Hardy boys, but when high explosives come into the picture, Frank and Joe figure there's more than a street fight at stake. The unknown enemy is willing to use deadly force to destroy the school, and the Hardys will have to get down to business—and give a lesson of their own . . . in *In Self-defense,* Case #45 in The Hardy Boys Casefiles™.